'Sandra! Dance for us. Dance for us, Sandra!'

A dozen different voices took up the cry in the crowded studio.

It was nearing midnight. One of the frequent parties given by Hugh Lancaster, the well-known artist, was at its height. The long, low, irregular room was full of people; men and women, mostly in fancy dress. A dark, electric-looking young man played a piano at one end of the studio. The windows were open, for it was a warm spring night.

Hugh Lancaster's studio parties were always good fun.

He had money; he was an attractive man and a good painter. The walls were hung with his sketches. Most of them black-and-white drawings of a girl's head. Always the same head. Beautiful, flawless features, curling hair, a gay provocative mouth. Sketches of Sandra,

1

Lancaster's favourite model.

Everybody shouted for Sandra now. 'Dance for us ... Sandy, darling ... do!'

On a raised dais at the end of the studio stood a girl. Her frock of gold tissue moulded her figure to the waist, where the gleaming, shimmering fabric flared into folds. Lissom, seductive, with her white slender arms, her wonderfully poised head, she stood on tiptoe. She was the spirit of fun, the very essence of vitality and laughter. Sandra, the prettiest model in Chelsea. Sandra — spoiled, wilful, idolised and still charming; the most generous of them all Sandra whose heart was of gold ... who was as straight as a die. And every man in her little world knew it.

Nobody knew it better than Hugh Lancaster. He was madly in love with her. He had sketched her a thousand times, and as many times had begged for her kisses. But he never got more than a light, idle caress, or a flippant, half-tender, half-mocking word. All that any man could boast from Sandra Medway.

Lancaster sat on the dais at her feet, a goblet of champagne lifted towards her.

'Your health darling!' he whispered.

She laughed down at him. She was inclined to like him, this very good-looking artist with his ardent white face and fair, sleek head and dark blue eyes that burned with admiration for her. But she wished he wouldn't be quite so ardent.

'Darling!' he repeated, 'Dance for me.'

She let one hand rest carelessly on his fair head. Hugh Lancaster caught it, carried it to his lips — lips that throbbed. Sandra bit her lip. Everyone was looking. She supposed everyone knew Hugh was wildly in love.

She began to dance. The young man at the piano played for her, a wild Russian tune that suited her mood. She was swift, light, graceful, lovely to look upon. Hugh Lancaster's burning blue eyes never left her face. Sandra, maddeningly beautiful, the short upper lip showing a gleam of perfect teeth; her wide-set, dark eyes, exquisite hands and feet.

She danced feverishly, and when the

music ended, Hugh Lancaster leapt on to the dais, seized her whirling figure, and lifted her right up in his arms.

He carried her through the studio, triumphant.

'What I have I hold!' he cried.

Everybody laughed. But Sandra did not laugh, She could feel the mad thumping of the man's heart. It worried her. She did not want him to love her so much. She could not return his love in that way. Lancaster set her on her feel in the cooler, dimmer room next to the studio, where he had carried her, and held her close to him.

'Sandra. Oh, my darling I love you so. You're wonderful.'

She strained back from him. Somehow he made her afraid.

She was just Sandra ... an artist's model; an orphan, whose English father was dead, whose beautiful Russian mother had succumbed to the cruelties of Communism. She shared 'digs' in Chelsea with another girl. She had nothing, no one to live for but herself. And if she had secret ideals, a secret wish for a more domesticated life, for a cottage, a husband to adore, nobody knew that save Sandra.

She hid her troubles and her disappointments. She laughed her way through life. She tried to be nice to Hugh without giving him too much encouragement.

'Don't be so serious, Hugh,' she said, her cheeks burning from the pressure of his lips. 'Let's go back to the others.'

'Not till you've told me you love me, Sandra'

'I don't know that I do.'

'I could make you love me ...'

'Perhaps I don't want to love you.'

'Don't madden me, Sandra. Darling for heaven's sake.'

He sought her lips again. But she grew frightened of his intensity, and pushed him away.

'Oh you can't be so unkind,' he whispered brokenly. 'The other night you kissed me and —'

'Don't make me sorry for it,' she broke in coldly. 'Now, really, I'm going back to the others!'

She was sorry for him ... it was pity that made her kind. But there would have been nothing in Sandra's heart but contempt and white-hot rage if she had known that Lancaster was a married man. Nobody knew that. He had kept it very quiet. When he rented this studio flat, six mouths ago, Chelsea had received him as a bachelor. Not a soul in Sandra's circle guessed that down in Devon, in a quiet cottage, there was a trusting, charming young wife who worshipped him and contented herself with seeing him at week-ends.

It was part of Sandra's code never to get involved with a married man. She would never have forgiven Hugh Lancaster or herself if she had been aware of Mrs. Lancaster's existence.

She returned to the studio feeling worried about Hugh; wondering whether she would sit for him as usual tomorrow.

She walked to the door. A good-looking red-headed boy immediately sprang to her side. He was John Trent — a young painter with a growing reputation. Sandra had sat for him several times, and he had been in love with her for some time. She treated him as she treated the rest-frivolously, leading him on a little, but with a good, warm friendliness behind it all.

'Not going already, Sandra?'

'Yes John, I'm tired.'

'I've got my car outside. I'll drive you back.'

'Thanks,' she said gratefully.

Sandra was due at Lancaster's studio at ten o'clock. She had been engaged to pose for head and shoulders. She decided not to go, but an urgent message brought her to the studio against her will. Lancaster was in the silk dressing-gown in which he usually breakfasted. He looked ill and drawn, and his eyes were haggard. The moment Sandra entered the studio which he was pacing, he rushed to her side, and seized her hands.

'Oh, darling, I've been so unhappy!'

'Hugh — really — this can't go on,'

she began.

'Don't!' he broke in. 'Sandra. don't hurt me any more.'

'But I haven't hurt you. It's wrong-it's unjust of you to blame me if I cannot return your love!' she protested.

He looked at her with searching eyes. She was adorably pretty. Hugh Lancaster was so mad about this girl that he gave no thought to the young wife who had implicit faith in him, and worshipped him.

'Sandra, be all the more generous,' he said unsteadily, and tried to take her in his arms. 'Darling, please!'

'I can't, Hugh!'

With an effort, she wrenched herself from his grip.

'I can't stand this,' she stammered. 'I shan't ever come again ... really ... it's too much!'

She turned and ran from the studio. She was thoroughly upset, and all her colour had gone. Down one flight of stairs, leading out of the building, she almost collided with a man. It was Ivor

Payne, the pianist of last night.

'Hello Sandra. You and Lancaster squabbling?'

'What business is it of yours?' Sandra flashed.

Then she stopped. She and Ivor stared at each other — Ivor startled; Sandra white to the lips. A shot rang out ... echoed through the building. A revolver shot. And it came from the direction of Lancaster's studio.

'Good heavens, what's that?' whispered Ivor.

Sandra put her hand to her lips. Her dark eyes were full of fear. 'Oh!' she said under her breath. Then, simultaneously, they turned and ran up the stairs to Lancaster's studio.

Ivor flung open the studio door which was ajar. Lancaster lay on the floor, face downwards; a smoking revolver in the right hand, blood pouring from a wound in the head. He had shot himself. When they turned him over, they found that he was quite dead.

Sandra, white-faced, shivering, feeling

9

violently ill, looked from the rigid body of the painter to a young horrified face.

'Suicide!'

She sank into a chair, and put her face in her hands.

'Suicide,' repeated Ivor. 'Over you, I suppose.' And that was what the world said, later on that day. A terrible day which Sandra never forgot ... could never forget. It was too crowded with horrors and with reproaches which she did not deserve. Suicide ... because of her.

When Elsie Lancaster arrived on the scene Sandra's cup of misery was full to overflowing. She felt bitter indignation against the dead man for not being frank with her. She would never have flirted with him ... granted him one single kiss, had she known about his wife. And who would credit the truth ... the truth as it was? How she had tried to end the slight affair that had existed between them; how she had tried to make Lancaster sane and sensible.

His wife did not know. His wife, hearing of Sandra, believed that she was a reckless woman who had lured her husband to his doom.

Two people understood and defended her. John Trent, and Doria Howland, the girl with whom she shared rooms. Doria, who knew Sandra better than anybody and would have starved years ago but for her kindness and generosity, was well aware that the public disapproval was undeserved.

Time softens most things, and in Chelsea art studios, where life moves rapidly, things blow over and are quickly forgotten. Within a few weeks of the inquest the painters and their friends and models had forgotten Lancaster's suicide. Beautiful, brilliant, Sandra was welcomed whereever she went. She continued with her work. But she had not forgotten.

And then one day love came to her. Overwhelming, all embracing love which wiped out everything.

2

When Michael Hunt first saw Sandra, she was executing an exaggerated step with a young Russian ballet dancer, who was one of the habitues of John's studio.

Michael, after three years of hard work in the East, years of loneliness and isolation — for his work took him a great deal into the desert — was bewildered by night life in a Chelsea studio.

The free-and-easy atmosphere, the abandon of it all, amused him somewhat, for he was not a prig. But it shocked him a little, too. He regarded the girl on the dais, who was dancing exquisitely, her dark, curly head flung back.

Michael watched her intensely. He had never seen a girl more beautiful. She appealed to his senses. Yet the quality of recklessness in her destroyed his admiration a little. He turned to a man nearby.

'Who is that dancing?'

'That girl? Oh, that's Sandra, one of the most famous models in Chelsea.'

Michael moved nearer the dais, extinguished the cigarette he had been smoking, and went on watching. He had no idea why Sandra was the most famous model in Chelsea. He had been trekking across the desert when the British newspapers containing reports of the inquest were being read in Cairo.

She finished the dance, her slim, lissom body bent so far back in the arms of her partner that Michael wondered she did not break. How supple she was, and how lovely! He was not a man easily moved by women. Yet he stood there, staring at Sandra and realising that her allure was extraordinary.

Sandra sprang from her partner's arm and opened her large dark eyes. Laughing, she jumped down from the dais and ran straight into Michael.

'Oh, sorry —' she began with her low, rich laugh. Then paused. She found herself smiling up into the face of a very tall athletic-looking man whom she had not seen before. And it was a face which immediately intrigued her. Thin, burnt dark brown by tropic suns: stern-lipped, yet with charm about the grey-blue eyes that looked down at her questioningly. She said, in a changed voice: 'I beg your pardon.'

'Not at all,' said he. 'You are — Sandra?'

'Yes, I'm Sandra,' she said simply.

'Known only by that name?' He smiled, and it was a smile that made the rather serious face of the man entirely charming and boyish. It went straight to Sandra's heart.

'Medway is my other name. My father was English, my mother Russian. I was born and bred over here.'

'I see. And I'm Michael Hunt — a friend of John's.'

Somebody had put a record on the big radiogram. A waltz. Couples started to dance. Michael said:

'May I? I dance very badly ... don't get much chance ... but if you'll forgive me ...'

'I'd like to dance with you,' she said simply.

An amazing thrill shot through her when Michael put an arm lightly about her waist and guided her into the centre of the room. And the man, with that fragrant, seductively beautiful figure in his arms, found his blood running more warmly through his veins than it had ever run before. But Sandra didn't know that. He had perfect self-control. He was rather aloof, cool.

Sandra, used to flattery, to open admiration, sensed the coolness.

Acute depression suddenly seized her. When the waltz ended, she left Michael with a flippant word ... to hide her real feelings.

'You don't dance too badly you know ... Adieu I'm going to wake up the party now ...'

The next moment she was turning out all the lights like a mischievous child, and crying:

'Find your partners ... scramble for the next dance.'

15

There was much laughter and shouting. Michael smiled goodnaturedly and moved in and out of the pushing, laughing party. But his grey eyes were thoughtful. He was thinking of Sandra — Sandra, whose loveliness and allure had crept into his heart without his knowing it. He couldn't really approve of her. She was too gay, too wild. And what a pity ... for she was lovely, charming ... and he had never seen more beautiful; more tragic. Why tragic? What had happened in her life?

He was pushed and pulled in the midst of the scrambling crowd in pitch-blackness. Then he heard a low, gay laugh . . . and two velvet-smooth arms went round his neck.

'Don't know who my victim is, but here I am ...' said a low, sweet voice.

He knew immediately that it was Sandra. Impulsively his arms went round her, and he felt her fragrant breath on his cheek. He thought:

'She expects to be kissed, in this silly studio-game, I suppose. Oh, very well ...'

16

The next moment he was kissing, quite wildly, and against all his principles — the softest, most fascinating mouth he had ever touched.

The emotion that Sandra's kiss roused in him was tremendous. The light flashed on. She saw who it was who held her, who had kissed her so passionately. Saw his grey eyes regarding her rather solemnly and a little regretfully.

Sandra caught her breath and drew back from him.

'Oh!' she said. She went absolutely white. Michael wondered why. Then she laughed and moved away from him.

She didn't dance with him again. He went home, slightly bewildered, half inclined to disapprove of this fascinating Sandra and wholly unable to forget that moment in the darkness when he had held and kissed her.

Sandra went home alone. She, too, was unable to forget Michael's embrace.

But she believed that Michael of the brown, strong face and blue-grey, critical eyes regarded her as a girl whom one could treat lightly and with flippancy. And she hated the idea — hated it, because she knew that this Michael Hunt was the one man on earth who had ever moved her with a single kiss. In other words, she was in love. And she would probably never see him again.

But she found that she did see Michael again. She saw him several times. He was in John's studio two or three mornings while she posed for the painter. She who could pose exquisitely, indifferent to most staring eyes, found herself nervous, embarrassed, flushing because Michael's serious, handsome eyes were watching her.

She tried to be gay and flippant, and failed miserably. She lapsed into silence in his presence. Every time he met her he found something new and intriguing about this lovely model. He had only intended staying in town a week. He stayed two. And every day he ran up against Sandra.

The deeper Sandra fell in love with him, the more shy she was, the more reticent in his presence. Her very shyness fascinated Michael. He was altogether enchanted by her before his fortnight's holiday in Chelsea ended.

There came an afternoon when John Trent held a little tea-party for three in his studio. Sandra was asked, and she found that Michael and herself were John's guests. And soon after tea John had a pressing engagement. Sandra and Michael were left alone.

'What are you thinking about?' asked Michael.

'Nothing,' she said. Then stood up, her cheeks burning. 'I must go home.'

'Home already?' Michael threw away his cigarette-end and also stood up. 'But why? Won't you stay and talk to me?'

'No,' she said under her breath.

'Sandra,' he said with a laugh, 'I believe you dislike me.'

She tried to answer and could not. Her heart beat frantically. She seized her hat and crushed it down on her curls.

'Well by-bye —' she began.

Then suddenly there leapt in Michael

19

a fierce flame. He seized her in his arms and crushed her close to him.

'You shan't go. You shan't dislike me, Sandra. I love you ... love you ... Do you hear? I've never loved any other woman. But I love you. Sandra listen to me-look at me!

She trembled in the strength of that embrace.

'I love you — I'm mad about you!' he said huskily. 'Sandra, Sandra — my darling — don't you care?'

She gave a little sob, and surrendered blindly, both arms locked about his neck.

'Oh, Michael, I love you so! Don't you know? Haven't you guessed? Oh, my darling ...'

The twilight deepened. It was almost dark in John's charming studio. Sandra and Michael kissed and kissed again. Then he said very tenderly: 'Sweet, when will you marry me?'

Sandra lifted her dark eyes to his, her whole face transfigured. The old Sandra, the inconsequent flirt, the gay coquette of Chelsea, had died. There was born a new Sandra — sweet, humble, yielding, ready to live and die for this man.

'Oh, Michael,' she said, 'am I good enough for you?'

'Why not? You've never done anything really wrong, my dear ...'

'No,' she whispered, and put her lips to one of his brown, warm hands. But her slim body suddenly trembled and her soul was sick within her at the memory of Hugh Lancaster.

3

Sandra was married to Michael by special licence, one week later. A delicious, delirious week for her. It was goodbye to the old life in Chelsea, the old work; the old friends. Two people, at least, were genuinely happy for her. John Trent, and Sandra's one woman friend — Doria. All Sandra's slender savings went towards a modest trousseau. Michael smiled tenderly at that, and said: 'Don't mind about new clothes. You look adorable as you are, and I'll buy you all the clothes you want in Paris — later on.'

Sandra only woke up, then, to the fact that Michael was quite a rich man; managing director of a firm of contractors in Cairo. Money meant nothing to her. She was so divinely happy with him; so tremendously in love. It was his love ... himself ... that Sandra wanted, and nothing, nobody else.

Michael, equally happy in his new love

which seemed to fill his whole life, was a masterful and passionate lover.

'I want you to myself ... you and only you,' he told her, on the eve of their wedding. 'Let's get a passport for you — I've got one — and fly to Paris after our marriage and stay there, lost to the world that knows us both, for three weeks.'

'Darling, it would be heavenly.'

'We'll do it, then. I've got a sister down in Devon I must see some time soon-but she doesn't realise I'm back yet. It'll be time enough when our honeymoon is over.'

So happy were they in Paris, Sandra had a queer dread of leaving it; almost a presentiment that something might happen to spoil things. She had no wish to go back to England where she had been Sandra, the artist's model.

Michael, with some month's leave before him, had no more wish than she to return to England, and duty-calls to his relatives. So they did not go back to London. When they left Paris, they went on to Italy, then to Spain.

They were more than ever passionate lovers when their golden honeymoon ended, and they returned to London in December. They went to a quiet hotel in Knightsbridge on the night of their return. And the next morning, for the first time since their marriage, they separated.

Michael found a letter waiting for him at his club. An urgent letter calling him down to Devon. A letter had been addressed to him in Cairo, had missed him, and been forwarded on to his club in London.

'It's my only sister,' he told Sandra. 'She's recently lost her husband. I feel a frightful brute. I knew nothing about it. She wrote to Cairo — this is the letter. It has followed me home. I must go and see her. I won't take you ... she doesn't even know I'm married ... but I'll try to bring her back with me to stay with us.'

'Darling, do,' said Sandra.

He thought about her without ceasing, all the way down to that remote little village in Devon. But, once there, he tried to concentrate on his sister, and her recent tragedy.

He found her pale, thin, listless; quite broken-hearted. 'Why, my dearest Elsie,' he said tenderly ... 'You do look ill. I'm most dreadfully sorry. I've been abroad ... only just got your letter. I'd no idea Hugh was ill. You didn't say ...'

'He was never ill,' broke in Michael's sister. 'Unless one can call it mental illness. Michael . . . poor Hugh committed suicide."

'Suicide,' repeated Michael. 'My dear! But why — why?'

'A woman,' said Mrs. Lancaster, bitterly.

'Elsie!' exclaimed Michael. 'This is frightful.'

Elsie Lancaster burst into tears. Clinging to her brother, she blurted out the whole story of Hugh's mad affair with an artists' model.

When she had finished, Michael jerked out: 'What was her name?'

'I don't remember her surname,' said Elsie with a sob. 'But she was known in those studios as Sandra.'

Silence. Michael stared at his sister. His face went ghastly white under the bronze. He repeated the name:

'Sandra! Oh, not Sandra'

'Yes ... a dark-eyed girl; pretty enough, but wicked to the core!' exclaimed Elsie. She went to a bureau and brought out some cuttings. 'I can show you all the newspaper reports. Look, here is her photograph. She was censured by the coroner. She ... Michael, what is it?'

For her brother had released her and dropped into a chair and hidden his face in his shaking hands.

4

Sandra sat in the private sitting-room of the hotel in Knightsbridge, waiting for her husband to come back.

She was a little troubled, and walked impatiently up and down the small room, as the grey day lengthened, and there was no sign of Michael. He had said he would be back soon after lunch.

She had a particular longing for him to come back today, too. She had something so very important and particular to tell him. A sweet, thrilling secret to confide. She had waited until now to make sure. And now she was sure that there was going to be a baby.

When dusk came and Michael had not come back from Devon, Sandra grew worried. With an awful sinking feeling of the heart she asked herself if anything could have happened to him. She decided to telephone his club. Perhaps he had called in there on his way from the station, and they could relieve her mind and tell her he was all right.

The clerk who answered said politely: 'Mr. Hunt called in here some time ago.'

'Did he?' exclaimed Sandra, puzzled.

'Yes. He took some luggage which he had here, and we wired reservations for him at Newhaven. He was catching the night-boat to Dieppe.'

Sandra put a hand to her heart. It beat so fast it hurt her. She was utterly baffled and unspeakably hurt. Michael — going abroad — without her? Leaving on the boat-train tonight ... without one word of explanation ... What had happened?

Almost hysterical with fear, she put on her coat and hat and rushed downstairs into a taxi.

'Victoria Station . . . for the boat-train,' she said hoarsely.

At the barrier she found a stream of people passing through to the *Golden Arrow*. She searched the crowd with wild, dilated eyes.

And then she saw Michael ... the tall familiar figure in the dark grey suit which he had worn when he left her yesterday morning.

As he reached the barrier, Sandra rushed up to him and caught his arm, a sob of thankfulness escaping her.

'Oh, Michael ... thank God ... I've found you!' she said.

He turned and looked at her. To her dying day Sandra never forgot that look. It was one of such chill scorn, such bitter pain and reproach. Then silently he flung off her hand. She gasped and cried out:

'Michael ...!'

He passed straight by her, through the barrier, and down the platform ... disappearing in the crowd.

'Michael!' Sandra wailed the name. Then the busy scene of the station was blotted out. Darkness descended on her. She had fainted. And five minutes later, long before she was fully conscious again, the Paris train steamed out of Victoria Station.

Michael was going back East with the intention of remaining there, of never returning to England, of never seeing his wife again.

Her allure still held him. He crushed it down. He wanted her. He despised her. He despised himself for still wanting her.

Michael felt he could not bear to set eyes on her lovely treacherous face again. He left word with his bank to pay a certain sum of money to her quarterly. He was her husband. He would at least fulfil his financial responsibilities. But he hoped never to see her again.

But Michael was a bitterly unhappy, heavy-hearted man when he left England for Paris that starlit night.

Yet not so unhappy, so desperate as his young wife when she recovered and found herself lying in a waiting-room in the great unfriendly station.

She started up wildly; her face and hair wet. The woman-in-charge had been bathing her forehead with water. Pale as death, wild-eyed, Sandra tried to get on to her feet.

'Let me go.... Let me go to my husband!'

The woman pushed her gently back on the bench where she had been laid, propped up by a pillow.

'There, there, dear,' she said. 'No use. The boat-train's gone. It was the Arrow you were trying to catch, wasn't it?'

'Yes,' said Sandra, breathing very fast. 'Yes.'

'It's gone my dear,' said the woman, 'fifteen minutes ago.'

Sandra's large dark eyes held the expression of a trapped bird ... She was frantic with pain and grief. With her hand to her throbbing head she could see Michael, pushing his way through the barrier, giving her that cold, terrible look; avoiding her, ignoring her, leaving her!

She managed to convince the attendant that she would be all right and left the waiting-room.

She went back to her hotel like one in a daze. She was numb with pain, with grief, and completely puzzled. She could not think why Michael had done this thing to her.

She walked drearily into her bedroom. He had evidently made up his mind to rush away without seeing her again. He had left so many of his things. His brushes, his cigarette case on the dressing-table.

He had gone . . . left her . . . he was on his way to the Continent. Why? Why? Why?

Sandra flung herself down on the bed. 'I can't bear it!' she moaned to herself. And she rushed to the telephone and called up John Trent's number. He was in, had just come home from a dinner.

'Hello,' he said cheerfully. 'How are you? How's Michael?'

Her voice, hoarse with sobs, answered:

'John ... John, he's gone ... gone ... Left me!'

'Left you!' repeated the artist amazedly. 'Good heavens. when ... why?'

'I don't know,' said Sandra in a frantic voice. 'I don't know. It's killing me. I love him so. Oh, John!'

''I'll come round to you at once,' said John.

He rushed round to Sandra's hotel. He was horrified at the sight of her ravaged young face. He held one of her cold hands between his; questioned her, tried to get at the bottom of the mystery, and confessed himself utterly bewildered.

'It beats me, Sandra,' he said. 'Why, Michael adored you!"

'I know,' she said tragically. 'And tonight ... on the platform ... he gave me a terrible look ... and just ignored me. And he's gone ... gone. And at the Club, they say he's picking up a boat at Cherbourg . . . and going back to Egypt.'

'It's incredible.' said John.

'Why has he done it?' she cried wildly. 'I've done nothing. Has anyoue told him about the dreadful Lancaster case? But who? He went to Devon to his sister. She wouldn't have said a word, wouldn't know me.'

'Get hold of the sister,' advised John.

'I don't even know her address ... or her name. Michael always spoke of her as 'my sister'. He hardly ever discussed her.'

She began to cry again, heart-brokenly. The artist, deeply distressed on her behalf, did his best to comfort her. But he was as puzzled as herself.

He ended by advising her to follow Michael out East.

'I know his bank in Cairo ... go there ... find out where, he is ... Hang it, he has done an unpardonable thing in leaving you alone like this, and you must see him ... you've a right to see him and demand an explanation.'

'There must be, a reason why he's done it, and surely when we meet, he'll tell me ... put things right,' Sandra said brokenly.

5

But Sandra's lucky star had set A fresh disaster befell her *en route* for Egypt.

She discovered, definitely, that Michael had returned to Cairo, because she applied to his bank who gave her that news, and also told her there would be a certain amount of money to her credit to be drawn quarterly. The money did not matter. Sandra would rather have followed him barefooted than remain with a fortune without him. But she drew what money was necessary to see her through to Egypt.

With nothing but the burning desire to find her husband, she boarded the liner which was to take her on that ten-days' voyage to Alexandria. On the second day out, a storm came up. Most of the passengers kept to their cabins. But Sandra, restless, feverish with tragic impatience of mind, could not sleep. She paced the decks outside in the wind and the rain.

The lashing rain made the deck slippery, Sandra was blown like a leaf and before she could save herself, fell heavily. A passing sailor picked her up and gave her into the care of a stewardess.

For the rest of the voyage, which was passed in calm, exquisite weather with a glass-like blue sea and cloudless sky, Sandra was seriously ill. With that illness passed her dear hopes of bearing Michael's son. When she reached Alexandria, she was well again, but she knew that she would not be the mother of a child. With the end of that particular hope came a crushing sense of loneliness; of bitter loss. It had been a divine link with him.

She reached Cairo at last, a pale, fragile ghost of the old Sandra; all eyes, dark, shadowy, tragic under the sweeping lashes; consumed with a fever of longing to see her husband again.

She found a quiet, moderately cheap hotel in the Heliopolis district. She sat awhile after dinner, drinking coffee.

Then restless, miserable, Sandra put a

scarf over her head and walked through the streets to try to make herself dead tired so that she would sleep.

An Egyptian with a cruel, bold face saw the hauntingly lovely eyes and the wonderful figure and followed her.

After a while, Sandra realised that she was being followed. She tried to walk faster, to escape the man. He dogged her footsteps. Sandra's heart began to beat fast with nervousness. She lost herself … half ran down a narrow street whence came the sound of music and singing.

She saw a place with a lighted sign: 'The Crescent Moon Café.' It seemed to her a refuge. Panting she ran into the place through a beaded curtain. She found herself in a room full of small tables round a floor on which couples were dancing.

It was a café where a woman might expect a man to speak to her. Nobody took any notice of such occurrence there. But Sandra did not know. She thought she would sit down, order some coffee and be safe from her persecutor.

He came in, saw the English girl with the lovely face, and eagerly joined her at her table.

He said something to her in Arabic. She did not understand. Terrified, she rose to her feet. The Egyptian immediately seized her wrists and tried to make her dance with him. He laughed and kissed her hair. Then Sandra screamed.

'Don't ... Oh, don't! Leave me alone! Help! Help!'

An Englishman heard that cry. At once he turned towards the café and rushed in.

'What's all this ... ? he began.

He paused. He saw an Egyptian trying to hold the slender, struggling figure of a girl in a black lace dress. The girl turned her face to him.

'Help!' she sobbed.

The man saw that beautiful, terrified face ... saw and recognised it. He gave a hoarse cry:

'Sandra!'

Sandra turned right round. The Egyptian shrugged his shoulders and released her. She put her hands to her burning cheeks and stared incredulously at the tall, bronzed Englishman with the stern grey eyes. Then, with her whole soul in her eyes, she flung herself at him.

'Michael ... it's you!'

She clung to his arm, tears pouring down her face.

'Oh, Michael, take me out of here!'

'You ought not to be in here,' he said, and turned towards the exit. 'Please follow me.'

Humbly she went with him, adoring him with all her eyes. If only he wouldn't look at her as though he detested her. Outside in the starlit street he faced her.

'What are you doing in Egypt, Sandra?'

'I followed you, Michael,' she said in a choking voice. 'I had to come. Oh, why did you desert me after our honeymoon ... ignored me when I called you at the station that day? Michael, you've broken my heart. But I love you so ... I had to follow ... to find you. Michael, tell me why you did this thing?'

He bit his lip. Her white tragic young face, her clinging fingers unnerved him. He reminded himself that she was unscrupulous and a clever actress. He said very grimly:

'We can't have a scene here. Come back to my flat.'

A moment later he signalled to a passing taxi, and was driving through the streets with her to his flat.

It was a flat which he occupied when he was not actually at his irrigation work on the fringe of the desert. A very beautiful place with a sitting-room with two balconies overlooking the Nile.

Michael had bought the place as it stood, two years ago, from an Egyptian pasha who was leaving Cairo.

In the exotic lounge, he faced the girl he had come out here to escape, and strove to remember his broken-hearted, lonely sister ... and Hugh Lancaster who was dead ... striving not to allow himself to be swayed by Sandra's beauty or charm. His one bitter wish was to punish her for her sins.

40

She flung herself at him, overwhelmed with happiness.

'Oh, Michael ... take me, hold me ... tell me it has been a ghastly nightmare. Please, please, darling, don't torture me any more. I love you ... adore you ... Oh, you know it!'

'Perhaps you love me a little more than you loved the unhappy man whom you drove to his death?' he said in an icy voice.

Sandra's heart jumped. Her cheeks flushed scarlet. Then she grew deadly pale. She said in a strangled voice:

'So, it's that ... I might have known. You found out about — Hugh Lancaster.'

'Yes,' said Michael in the same frozen voice. 'I visited my sister, Elsie, in Devon. She told me everything.'

'What does your sister know?' cried Sandra wildly.

'More than most people. She was Hugh Lancaster's wife!'

'Your sister ... was his wife?' gasped Sandra.

41

'Yes. A peculiar coincidence, Sandra. But that is the grim truth. My sister was Mrs. Lancaster. I saw her ... broken-hearted ... alone ... her life wrecked through your heartless conduct. You — you drove Lancaster to suicide.'

'Michael, stop saying those dreadful things to me.'

'You're not fit to live,' he flung at her bitterly. 'Do you deny that you drove my brother-in-law to suicide?'

'I don't deny that he killed himself ... because I refused his love. But I ... didn't love him. Why should I have given in to him?' she asked, with a sob. 'And I didn't even know he was married.'

'I can't believe that, Sandra.'

'It's true. It's true. Oh, Michael, I'm not as bad as you think!'

'Worse,' he said scornfully.

'Michael, whatever happened in the past ... I loved you,' she whispered. 'Oh, you'll never, never know how much I love you still in spite of all you've said to me.'

He looked down at her. He saw that

she had changed, seemed ill, broken, suffering. He knew she spoke the truth when she said that she loved him. Perhaps he could use that very love as a means of making her pay. Every time he thought of his broken-hearted widowed sister, he writhed with longing to make Sandra pay.

'I left you because I hated and despised you for what you are,' he said. 'Perhaps I was foolish. That wouldn't punish a woman like you. Perhaps it would hurt you more if I kept you here with me ... showed you day and night how I despise you.'

But the jibe did not hurt her. She was too broken with love, and longing. To his amazement she flung herself into his arms.

'Yes, yes, let me stay, Michael. ... Oh, let me stay. I can't bear to be parted from you. I do love you so. I'll make you love me again. Oh, you must, you shall!'

He unwound her arms from his neck and held her away from him. He looked at her with cold scorn.

'You'll never make me love you again as long as you live, Sandra. I never did love you.'

'Michael ... !' the cry was wrung from her.

'Never,' he added. 'I knew what you were ... yes, I knew all the time. I only went through that marriage farce with you to make you suffer in the way you made my sister suffer.'

'Michael . . . do you mean I ... I'm not your wife? That our marriage wasn't legal?'

For an instant Michael wavered. Then he laughed and lied deliberately:

'Yes. I mean — just that. You are not my wife at all!' Sandra put both hands to her ears.

'No,' she said under her breath, 'I don't believe it!'

'I'm sorry,' he said, 'but it's quite true.'

She gasped and flung out a hand.

'Michael ... you can't mean it! You're saying that to frighten me — hurt me. How can it be true? We were married in a London Register Office ...' she broke off, choking.

'Oh, yes,' said Michael, flicking the ash from his cigarette, 'the marriage appeared legal enough. But the licence was a fake. Anyhow, I assure you — you are not my wife.'

Trembling violently, Sandra said:

'You did that ... faked our wedding ... knowing that I was the girl in the Lancaster case ... knowing about your sister? You did it all ... deliberately?'

'Quite. It seemed an excellent plan for punishing you, Sandra ... for making you suffer as you must have made my wretched brother-in-law suffer before he killed himself.'

She stood swaying a little ... hands clasped to her breast.

'If it is true,' she said slowly. 'That I am not your wife ... It means I ... I've been your ...'

'You needn't say it,' he broke in, avoiding her gaze; 'but that is what you have been.'

'I see,' she said in the same slow dull voice. 'Then I ... I'd better go away.'

Then Michael moved forward and, with a swift gesture, pulled her trembling figure into his arms. He held her close to him; gave a short laugh; then kissed her slim pale throat.

'Oh, no,' he said. 'I think not. Now you've come, my dear, you can stay. You've followed me to Egypt. Very well, you can remain in my flat and amuse me a little more.'

Of all the things he had said, that seemed to Sandra the most brutal and horrifying.

She strained away from him.

'No, Michael … no! … You're wrong this time. Nothing will induce me to stay with you if I am not your wife.'

'You're not asked, Sandra. You'll do as I choose.'

He pulled her closer. The lure of Sandra's beauty was still strong upon him, and while he despised her, he wanted her.

'I'm quite glad you came, Sandra,' he said with a harsh laugh. 'You still amuse me. There isn't a girl in Egypt with such

46

eyes, such lips, such hair …'

She began to sob drearily.

'Michael, you've broken my heart … you've punished me enough … and I don't deserve it.'

'You deserve all that you get,' he broke in. 'And if I've broken your heart — good! I've avenged Lancaster and Elsie.'

'Then let me go . . .'

His arms tightened about her.

'No. Your punishment has only begun.'

'But don't you see what you are doing to me?' she sobbed. 'I'm not you wife … you are insulting me hideously.'

He did not answer. He knew that she was his wife. He knew, too, that this was a subtle method of torture. The insults she imagined he heaped on to her were more effective than any other punishment could have been.

47

6

Next morning Sandra found herself alone in Michael's flat. Long before she had wakened from a restless, unhappy sleep, he had risen and dressed and gone out riding. When he came back, two of his Arab servants had carried out his orders and collected Sandra's luggage from her hotel.

He came to her bedside and spoke to her.

'Your luggage is here,' he greeted her. 'I sent for it. I have also sent for a woman to wait on you. She will arrive later. Breakfast is served on the balcony.'

'Michael,' Sandra said, 'you forced me to stay with you last night. But I shall not stay another hour in your flat. You have no right to make me stay. I am not your wife.'

'You don't wish to live with me?'

'No, no,' she said huskily, her face and throat burning. 'I want to go ... to go home ... never to see you again.'

'Well, I'm not going to let you go, Sandra,' he said. 'Get dressed and join me on the balcony.'

After he had left her, she lay face downwards on the big bed, shuddering with sobs. But only for a moment. Then a wild feeling of resentment flared up in her. She would not stay and be so hurt, so degraded by him.

Rapidly she unpacked a suitcase and found a suit, a white cotton frock and wide-brimmed tuscan straw hat. Swiftly, she washed, dressed. Then she ran to the bedroom door.

She was going — going away.

She found the door locked. She ran feverishly into the adjoining sitting-room. That door yielded to her touch. She found herself in a long white corridor. At the end was the front door. But before this an Arab boy, in white galabieh, was standing sentinel.

'Let me get by ... open that door,' Sandra stammered. The Arab saluted gravely, but shook his head.

'It is not permitted, Madame,' he said in good English.

Indignant, Sandra discovered that she was nothing but a prisoner in this flat. She found her way to the balcony. There, in the sunlight, Michael sat in a low basket chair.

'Michael,' said Sandra in a quivering voice, 'tell your Arab servant to let me out of this flat — at once.'

He looked up at her calmly.

'Sorry,' he said. 'Selim is carrying out my orders. You are not permitted to leave this flat.'

She gasped; her heart beat frantically fast.

'But — but it's outrageous. You can't keep me here against my will.'

'Oh, yes, I can. My word is law with all my servants.'

She put her hand to her throat.

'Michael, haven't you tortured me enough? Let me go.'

'No. Please sit down quietly and have your breakfast, Sandra.'

She dropped into the chair indicated,

and obeyed.

He left the flat, an hour later, on business. He was not due in the desert for another fortnight. He had work in the company's offices in Cairo.

Michael did not return to the flat until late in the afternoon. He had been working hard. He was in a bad humour and the thought of Sandra had worried him ... made him feel a brute ... and the reaction was that he became doubly brutal.

He took a special delight in hurting her that evening. Jeered at all the things they had done together on the Continent; mocked at Sandra's loveliest memories until she was smarting under the taunts.

'Oh, leave me alone ... you have no right to make everything seem so ... beastly!' she choked.

He laughed and caught her in his arms.

'No matter. There is no such thing as love or fidelity. Only beauty and emotion ... and we are alone ... and this is Egypt ... and we'll pretend this is our second honeymoon ...'

He kissed her, still laughing. And Sandra went down, down, into the depths of that agony he was making for her, and wondered how long it would be before her love for him changed to hatred.

The days passed. Lonely, unhappy days when Sandra was a prisoner in the flat. Bitter days when she was swept along on the tide of his cruelty, his vengeance.

She masked her despair with nonchalant defiance. She put on her prettiest frocks, flung herself into what gaiety Cairo offered. Went with Michael everywhere ... danced ...tried to make herself, as well as Michael, believe she didn't care.

There came a night when she and Michael were in a well-known dance club in Cairo ... Michael was called away on the telephone by a business friend. Sandra was left alone. But not for long. A tall fair Englishman with very blue eyes crossed the polished floor and spoke to her. He had been watching her — immensely attracted by her beauty.

'Will you dance with me?' he asked in French, not knowing her nationality.

'We will have this one, if you like,' she said in English.

'Thank you,' he said. 'So you are English too.'

'Half Russian,' she smiled wearily. He put an arm about her. He drew the graceful figure close. He danced well.

'Tell me your name,' he murmured.

'It is Sandra,' she said.

'My name is Bentley. Victor Bentley.'

'You live in Cairo?' she asked.

'Never in any one place for long. I am a wanderer. I have a lot of money and nothing to do ... but wait for the gods to offer me what they have offered tonight — this dance — with Sandra!'

His voice was eager, smooth. Sandra could tell that he was greatly attracted by her. His admiration bored her. But the thought leapt into her mind:

'This man might help me escape ... from Michael.'

'Are you married?' he asked.

'No,' she said. 'I am — not married.'

'Then who is the big fellow you are with?'

Sandra looked over Victor Bentley's shoulder and saw that Michael had returned to their table. He was standing there, hands clenched at his sides, face white, eyes dark with rage ... watching her dance. Then he strode straight across the room and tore her out of Bentley's arms.

The three of them stood a little to one side of the room.

Sandra spoke first:

'How dare you do that?'

'How dare you dance with a stranger in this club?' came through Michael's set teeth, his eyes glowering at her. 'Put on your coat and come home at once, Sandra.'

Victor Bentley spoke:

'If you'll pardon me ...' he began.

Michael turned on him savagely.

'I pardon you nothing. You had no right to speak to my wife.'

'Mr. Bentley had every right to speak to me. I wanted him to!' Sandra blazed.

Victor Bentley looked at her with admiration.

'Oh, so you wanted him to. How enlightening,' said Michael. 'Put on your coat and come home, Sandra.'

Sandra walked to the table.

'Very well. I'll go home,' she said.

Michael looked Victor Bentley straight in the eyes.

'Speak to my wife again, and I'll knock your damned head off,' he said.

Bentley's face went crimson. But anger did not prevent him from being a coward. He shrugged his shoulders and moved away.

But as he moved across the shining dance-floor, he felt a light touch on his arm. He turned and saw Sandra.

'Listen,' she said breathlessly. 'I ... need a friend ... I can't explain ... he will make another scene. But will you help me ... please ...'

Bentley sensed an intrigue and a very agreeable one.

'Of course I'll help you,' he said, his olive face eager. 'Tell me how ... when

... where ...'

'Tomorrow morning ... I'll be on the balcony of our flat at eleven. He goes to his office then ... you see?'

She hastily whispered the address.

Victor Bentley watched the couple leave the café. He had not been so intrigued or excited for years. Sandra was not only beautiful but wildly fascinating.

In the taxi driving back to their flat, there was an uncomfortable silence between Sandra and Michael.

At eleven o'clock next morning Sandra hastened to the balcony and stood a moment in the hot sunlight. Her heart shook. Michael had gone. She was a prisoner, because of his faithful Arab servants. But there was Victor Bentley. Would he keep his promise and come ... help her to escape?

She looked down at the white street, and suddenly bit her lower lip hard with excitement. A slim, graceful figure in a cool linen suit, with a green hat on his sleek head, came swinging along. She recognised Bentley, her dance partner of last night.

He saw her on the balcony and paused below.

'Sandra!' he cried softly.

'So you've come,' she breathed leaning down to him.

'Of course. Can't you come down?'

'No. There are Arabs at all doors ... my ... husband's servants.'

Victor Bentley considered this, frowning. At length he said:

'Surely you — an English girl — won't stay with a fellow who behaves like a barbarian?'

'No,' said Sandra.

'You must hate him,' said Bentley.

'Perhaps I do hate him. Anyhow, I want to get away. Listen,' she breathed, leaning over the balcony. 'If you are my friend ...'

'More than a friend,' he broke in eagerly.

'No, no — I want only friendship,' said Sandra.

'As you wish,' said Bentley bowing. But he knew, definitely, that he would never be content with friendship.

'What do you suggest?' Sandra panted. 'Quick — we must be quick. These Arabs spy ...'

'Is there always an Arab at the door?' he asked.

'Until midday, when the servants have food. Then they disappear. But the door is locked.'

'From the outside?'

'Yes.'

'Good. Then at midday I will be there-with my revolver. I shall level it at the fellow's head and keep him covered until you're out of that flat. I've got a villa in Heliopolis. You shall come there. Later we will go down the Nile. I have a daha-beeyah ... my own boat ...'

Sandra was not so sure about that. But for the moment she must use this man to her own ends. And her one fervent ambition was to get away from Michael.

'Very well,' she said breathlessly.

Sandra waved him farewell, and

returned to the cool of the flat. She waited until her maid retired to the servants' compound and then packed a suitcase with the things she had brought with her from England.

Midday came. Sandra, nervous, worried and acutely miserable, slipped into the hall as the hour struck and the Arab boy prepared to go to his lunch.

He did not see her emerge, very softly, from the bedroom. With his back to her he opened the hall door. He was astonished and terrified to find himself confronted by the shining barrel of an automatic. A cool, dark-eyed young man spoke to him in Arabic:

'Get out ... and a curse upon you if you attempt to interfere.'

The boy gasped. He stood aside, shivering. Victor Bentley called:

'Sandra!'

She came running along, carrying her suitcase, one hand to pulsing throat. He smiled into her eyes, took the case, and put the automatic in his pocket.

The next moment they were out of the

white building and in a long, sleek car with a silver bonnet. Victor's car, driven by an Egyptian chauffeur. Bentley did not lack means.

He smiled down at Sandra.

Sandra bowed her head. Her lips trembled. She had escaped from Michael's flat. Yet she felt no triumph. And what, after all, did she know of this man? He was a stranger to her.

Bentley guessed what was in her mind.

'No need to be scared. Sandra. You can trust me.'

Sandra swallowed hard.

'Oh ... all right. Thank you. But I'd rather go to an hotel.'

'Oh, no, my villa is so much more comfortable,' he broke in smoothly. 'And I have a housekeeper ... a Frenchwoman ... Madame Marque. She will chaperon you.'

Sandra smiled faintly. She tried to cheer up.

She talked and laughed a trifle nervously and with obvious strain during the drive to Bentley's villa. He was enchanted by her.

Sandra found the villa an exquisite place, surrounded by an exotic Eastern garden.

Sandra was received with great courtesy by the French housekeeper, Madame Marque, a thin, sharp-featured woman with snapping black eyes and an obvious adoration for her master.

Sandra was given no chance to regret accepting Victor's hospitality, and it was a relief to sit and talk to a man who did not wish to torture or humiliate her. She began to bask, very humanly and naturally, in the sunshine of a little homage and attention, and to think with bitter resentment of Michael.

When Victor mentioned such words as 'divorce' or 'legal separation' she flushed but did not undeceive him. For her own sake she could not bring herself to tell Victor that she was indeed, free, and was not Michael's wife.

But her rest did not last long. Later that night Michael broke like a wrathful thunderbolt upon the temporary peace.

Sandra knew, before his car reached the villa, that he was coming. She heard the familiar horn.

She sprang up and clutched Victor's arm.

'Oh ... that's ... that's my husband's car ... I know that horn — I'd know it anywhere.'

Victor stood up. His eyes narrowed.

'So he's traced us, has he? Clever of him. Well what are you going to do, Sandra? You won't give in? You'll face things, won't you? You're not going to let the fellow bully you?'

'No,' whispered Sandra.

'Very well,' said Victor. 'We'll tell him to go to the devil.'

The car drew up before the villa. Sandra said to Victor:

'I want him to see I don't care ... I want to be gay, dancing. Put on a record-quickly ... Dance with me!'

When Michael entered the villa he found himself in a very exotic lounge, with polished floor and gilt pillars. A gay lilt came from the radiogram.

And Michael saw his wife in the arms of Victor Bentley. They were dancing in the lounge, laughing at each other.

For a moment Michael seemed to see red. When the mist cleared away he moved abruptly towards them. They stopped. There was tense silence. Victor Bentley said in a cold voice:

'What is the meaning of this intrusion? May I ask what you are doing in my house?'

Michael looked at him savagely.

'And may I ask what my wife is doing in your house?'

'And may I ask what right you have to come here and make this scene?' demanded Sandra.

He gripped her arm.

'Sandra, last night you came with me when I told you. You are coming tonight. You little fool. Don't you know you are in the villa of the most notorious man in Cairo? Oh, I soon found out where you'd got to. I recognised Bentley from the description my Arab gave me.'

'One moment,' broke in Bentley

with a drawl. 'It's all very well, Hunt, adopting that tyrannical, bullying attitude to your — er — wife. But she happens to have come away with me of her own free will, and if she chooses to remain with me ...'

'Yes, yes; Victor is right,' came from Sandra feverishly. She was not going to be beaten by Michael this time. Deliberately she took Victor's arm and clung to it. 'I have chosen to come here, and here I stay.'

'Not if I tell you to come back,' said Michael.

Temper, passionate, defiant, flared in her.

'We'll put an end to this farce?' she said breathlessly.

'I'm going to let Victor know the truth now. You have no authority over me at all. I am not your wife!'

'Ah!' said Victor softly, raising his brows.

Michael stood silent aghast. And suddenly he realised what he had done when he had told Sandra that lie in order to punish her.

At first he was inclined to tell her the truth, but on second thoughts he kept silent.

Victor Bentley was the first to speak.

'Why, my dear,' he murmured. 'I had no idea ...Why didn't you tell me? Under the circumstances this fellow has no right to order you about — none at all!'

'No, none!' said Sandra breathlessly. 'I'm not his wife.'

It hurt her desperately to stand there at the side of a man like Bentley who meant nothing to her and declare to him that Michael was not her husband.

'You had better go,' she said, looking at Michael with a wild unnatural light in her great dark eyes. 'Go and don't ever bother about me again. Forget me. Forget that I exist. I shall do the same about you.'

Michael gave her one long, bitter look, then turned and strode from the room.

Sandra and Victor stood listening. They heard the hum of a motor car break the stillness of the Egyptian night, then die away. Michael had gone.

Victor Bentley rubbed his hands together. An expression of extreme satisfaction was written over his handsome dissipated face. He looked at Sandra. She had hidden her eyes with her two slim, shaking hands.

He spoke to her softly:

'Sandra. You aren't crying, are you? You don't regret that man, surely!'

She let her hands drop. The face she lifted to him was white.

'I — love him,' she said.

So simply, so poignantly she said it. It would have touched the heart of any man but Bentley. He was beyond touching. A blase, cynical, sardonic creature without faith in life; without any genuine feelings. Amusement and luxury were the gods of his religion. He shrugged his shoulders and smiled at Sandra.

'Oh, my dear! One loves. One gets over it and loves someone else. That's life!'

'But that's not the way I love,' said Sandra.

She fell forward on the divan beside

her, her arms outstretched, her face buried in the cushions, agonised with grief. Victor Bentley frowned, lit a cigarette, smoked in silence a moment and let her cry.

'Do her good and get it over,' he thought contemptuously.

Gradually the violence of her grief subsided. Worn out, exhausted with emotion, she lay motionless, her face still hidden.

Then she felt a touch on her shoulder.

'That's better. No more weeping. You have the world before you. Everything that you want can be yours, *ma mie*!'

She raised herself and sat upright, looking up at the man whose existence she had almost forgotten. He smiled at her, his lids narrowed, a queer sardonic look on his face. He bent over her and tried to take her hands.

'Come,' he whispered. 'Forget sorrow. You are here with me Sandra and the night is yet young. Come out into my beautiful gardens. It is divine in the moonlight. Come to the Cypress walk ...

down to the lily pond ... and let us both forget the world and think only of each other.'

Sandra awoke, with a violent start, to the realisation that this man was trying to make love to her. She drew her hands sharply away.

'Please leave me alone, Victor.'

An ugly look replaced the fervour in his eyes.

'Oh, come, Sandra,' he said. 'You can't treat me like that. You have come here as my guest, accepted my hospitality and asked me to take you away, and now you're being unkind ...'

'You don't understand,' she broke in. 'I know I asked you to help me escape from ... from him ... but I didn't mean ...'

'Never mind. You are here in my villa and you can repay my kindness to you by — being very kind to me!'

The significance of that, of the expression in his eyes, horrified her.

'Victor — please — I — if you'd order a car for me, I'd like to go at once,' she stammered.

'Go where?' He smiled scornfully.

'To an hotel ... oh, anywhere. But I realise now that I can't stay here any longer — in your villa.'

'But you're going to, Sandra!'

He bent down with an unexpected gesture and pulled her into his arms. He pressed a cheek against her hot, flushed, tear-wet young face.

She realised then as she trembled in Victor's arms, that she could not break utterly with Michael. She must get back to him, implore him to keep her with him, to protect her.

She felt Victor's breath on her cheeks.

'I won't kiss you ... you shan't touch me ... you shan't ...' she stammered.

Suddenly the man grew tired of the contest. He was not fond of scenes. This little wild-cat, Sandra, was spoiling everything. He grew angry with her, and released her with sudden violence.

'If that's how you feel — I'm finished with you,' he said brutally.

She sprang to her feet.

'Well I do ... I do. I detest you. I despise you. I am going to leave your villa now, at once.'

'I regret you are not. There is an Egyptian at every door. You are not going to leave tonight.'

Sandra pressed ber hand to her aching head.

'Oh, why not? Why try and keep me knowing how I feel!'

He shrugged his shoulders.

'I have a hope that when tomorrow comes you may feel — a little more well-disposed.'

Sandra, very pale and scared, but more composed now, stood staring at him. He struck a little silver gong. A dark-eyed Egyptian woman, with sandals on her feet and wearing a white cotton burnous, padded in and greeted Victor as though she were his slave, almost touching the ground with her forehead.

Victor spoke to her in dialect, then said to Sandra:

'Go with Cleo. She will take you to your room.'

Sandra was too exhausted, emotionally and physically, to argue or protest further. She would stay tonight. She was forced to stay. But tomorrow she would get away, go back to Michael.

She slept hardly at all that night in the exotic bedroom to which the maid, Cleo, conducted her. And she was awake, feverish, dry-eyed, heart-broken when the dawn came.

She dressed and prepared to leave Bentley's villa.

She expected to find escape difficult. But it was made extraordinarily easy for her.

Victor Bentley was warned by one of his servants, on night-watch, that his guest was leaving the villa. Swiftly he put on a silk dressing-gown and hurried to the hall where she was furtively trying to unlock the door.

She faced him bravely, although her heart pounded.

'Victor,' she said, 'Let me go ... please!'

Then he did the unexpected thing. He bowed and immediately opened the door for her.

'Please consider yourself absolutely free.'

'Thank you,' she faltered. 'You — do understand. I ... don't want your love!'

'You made that plain,' he said sarcastically.

'I ... I'm sorry,' she flushed and stammered.

'Don't apologise. It is I who should do that. I was mad last night, Sandra. Please forgive me ... and if you need my friendship again — ask for it.'

His voice was gentle and his attitude contrite and courteous.

He had thought things out and reflected that he would assume this pose of friendship and contrition and let her go. Later another, bigger chance would come his way. She would not repulse him next time.

7

Michael was sitting on the balcony of his flat, eating iced grapefruit, when he saw a shadow fall across the sunlit balustrade. He looked up sharply, then sprang to his feet.

Sandra stood before him. A pale, humble, abject Sandra with great beseeching eyes and a red mouth that quivered piteously.

'What are you doing here?' he demanded.

'Michael,' she said in a husky voice. 'Michael I've come back. Please let me stay. Oh, you must!'

He stared at her, amazed, speechless. He had suffered agonies of regret because his wife was what he believed her to be.

'Why have you come back here to me?' he said in a hard furious voice. 'I never wanted to see your treacherous face again when I said goodbye to you yesterday. Go away … before I kill you- and your lover.'

'I have no, lover. Michael — I have no lover.'

'That's a lie. What about Bentley?'

'He is not my lover. Michael. I swear it!'

'I don't believe you. You stayed with him last night.'

'It's not what you think, Michael.'

'I don't care,' he said savagely. 'I don't want you back.'

'Listen Michael. I know I'm not your wife; that I have no claim on you. But I must come back to you.'

To his dismay she burst into passionate, stormy weeping and clasped his hand with both hers; pressing it to her breast convulsively. Sandra, so proud, so defiant … to be reduced to this. Michael was profoundly astonished and a little touched.

Well — let her stay! He would not, could not drive her away — back to the embraces of Victor Bentley. But he was not going to soften, to unbend further than to allow her to stay here. Her punishment was by no means complete.

'Go to your room, Sandra,' he said. 'I've nothing to say to you. But stay here ... if you wish.'

There commenced another queer, stormy period for these two.

Gradually the ice about Michael's heart thawed. He grew tired of his tyranny, ashamed of his cruelty to her. He came, several times, to the pitch of telling her the truth, of saying :

'You are my wife ...'

And he knew that if he let himself go, he would add to those words :

'And I love you still ... I have never stopped loving you.'

But Sandra was chafing, growing daily, hourly more impatient and again more resentful.

One night Michael left her alone in the flat, having left Cairo suddenly on business in Alexandria.

She went to bed early; tired out, miserable, wondering how long she could tolerate this life with Michael. She was just dozing fitfully, when she heard a light tap on her balcony window. She sprang up, wide awake; slipped on a silky wrap and shoes, and opened the windows wide. There, silhouetted against the vivid moonlight, was the slim, graceful figure of Victor Bentley. She had not set eyes on him since she had left his villa.

'What do you want?' she cried. He put his finger to his lips.

'Don't wake your husband. I want to talk to you, Sandra.

In an unguarded moment Sandra said: 'Michael is not here. He is away — in Alexandria.'

'Oh, better and better,' said Bentley.

Debonair, cool, in his white linen suit, he came towards her. But she waved him back.

'No — I can't allow this. It's impossible. Please go away.'

'Listen, Sandra,' he said. 'I haven't come to scare you or offend you. I'll go away at once if you like. But I want you to know this: I'm sorry for insulting you — which I did. I'm sorry Hunt should insult you by keeping you here like this. You're too beautiful, too good, too sweet for that. I've come tonight to make you an offer. I'm off up the Nile tomorrow. If you'll come with me, I'll marry you by special licence in Cairo — tomorrow.'

Sandra stared at him wild-eyed, breath fluttering. Marriage! Victor Bentley was offering her marriage.

She didn't love this man. But she wondered, suddenly, if she would be a fool to refuse such an offer. It would only serve Michael right if he returned from Alexandria to find her — Victor Bentley's wife!

Victor saw what lay in her eyes. He seized his opportunity. Quietly he said:

'You can trust me, Sandra. I won't ask for love until you say I can. Only marry me — come away with me. Let me take you away from this life of shame and tyranny.'

She said: 'Yes, yes. I want to get away. It is shameful … this tyranny … you are right.'

'Sandra!'

'Wait — let me think! Go in there ...'
She pointed to the archway leading from
her bedroom into the sitting-room. 'Wait
for me. I'll dress.'

Five minutes later she was dressed.

'He is in Alexandria on business,' she
said feverishly, her eyes gleaming with
excitement. 'He won't be back until
tomorrow.'

'But you mustn't stay here. You must
come at once. My dahabeeyah is waiting
on the river now ... ready to go.'

She paced up and down the room
without answering him for a moment.
She looked at the many little things
which reminded her of Michael. The old
bitter pain of loving him smote her.

But swamping it came the resentment;
the fierce, injured pride. She swung
round and looked at Victor Bentley.

'Very well. I will come with you,' she
said. 'I will leave this flat in case he comes
back; go to an hotel; marry you the first
thing in the morning, and then go up the
Nile with you.'

'Good!' said Victor Bentley.

'Victor,' Sandra said, 'I am going to give you a terrible lot ... by giving myself to you in marriage. I don't love you. I shall never love any man again. Michael was my lover. He let me down. So I'm leaving him. But you will be good to me, won't you?'

Bentley's eyes dropped before the clear candour of her gaze. He did mean to marry her, yes. He wanted her for his wife. But was he capable of being 'good' to any woman? No. He was selfish, worthless. He knew it.

'I adore you,' he said. 'I swear you'll never regret marrying me. I'll be good to you, Sandra. And you shall learn to forget this man. I'll teach you to care for me.'

She felt that she had burned her boats finally when she crept out of the flat into the gorgeous Egyptian starlight with Victor Bentley, carrying her case beside her.

There was a comfortable hotel close by, with a night porter on duty. Victor left Sandra there.

'I shall go back to the river,' he said.

'My villa is closed. My servants and my things are already on board. At eleven o'clock I shall call for you and we will go to the Cairo Register Office.'

'But the licence —' she began.

He gave a smile and tapped his pocket.

'Forgive me, adorable, but I took that out yesterday.'

'You were so sure I would come!' She frowned and flushed.

'I only hoped . . .' He smiled again.

'I'll forgive you,' she said. 'Yes, call for me in the morning.'

He left her. The night porter carried her suitcase into the hotel and showed her to a room. She slept, exhausted, dreamless, until she woke to see the sun streaming through the shutters and found that it was half-past nine.

She rose quickly, bathed and dressed.

She went downstairs and found Victor waiting for her. 'Sandra,' said Victor, taking her hand. 'You look beautiful ... I've been terrified you might change your mind.'

'I haven't changed it,' she said steadily.

'I shall marry you, Victor; and afterwards ... we will send Michael a telegram.'

Half-an-hour later she emerged from the Registrar's with a new ring on her finger, a circlet of tiny diamonds which Victor had chosen for her wedding ring. A certificate in her bag.

She went to the post office with the man she thought her husband. She wrote a telegram to Michael.

I married Victor Bentley this morning, and you will never see me again. Goodbye.
                              Sandra Bentley.

Sandra sent the wire.

That wire reached Michael half-an-hour after it was sent. He had arrived back from Alexandria unexpectedly soon. He walked into his flat calling his wife.

'Sandra! Sandra!'

There was a tenderness in his handsome eyes and an eager note in his voice which Sandra would have given her soul for in the past. He had thought

81

much about her in his absence. He had remembered not her misdeeds, but her sweetness and charm. He had made up his mind to start again, to give her another chance ... to grant their love a new lease of life.

Then a boy came running to him with a telegram. He took it, ripped it open. It was from Sandra. The words danced before him. The last message on earth that he expected.

I married Victor Bentley this morning ...

He read it twice, then crushed it into a ball and sat down.

Married to Bentley. Married! What a tragedy! Of course, she didn't know that she was his (Michael's) wife. He had told her that she was not. And this was where his lie had led her. She had committed bigamy ... with Victor Bentley.

Michael sprang up and hurled the crumpled wire on the floor. He was like one crazy with rage and — though he would not admit it — with jealousy. The idea of Sandra, his wife, in the arms of Bentley, infuriated him. But she should not defeat him; that was unthinkable! Those two should not go away together, laughing, crowing over him.

He rang a bell, his face livid under the tan.

'Pack my things,' he said. 'Get out my car.'

Within a quarter of an hour he had travelled to Victor Bentley's villa. He found it shuttered and deserted, except for an old Arab in the servants' quarters.

'Where is your master?' Michael demanded of him.

'He has gone,' said the old man.

'Gone where?'

'I know not, Excellency,' said the Arab.

'You must have some idea,' said Michael impatiently.

'I do not know. Save that the master travels up the Nile, Excellency, in his boat.'

That was enough. Michael turned from him and leaped into his car again.

'Drive to the river,' he bade the Arab chauffeur. 'Fast … faster than the four winds of heaven.'

8

A golden moon upon the Nile. A hot, drowsy exotic atmosphere on Victor Bentley's boat, which moved slowly and smoothly down the greenly-brown waters of the loveliest river in the world.

Under a red canvas canopy, Sandra — who now thought herself Mrs. Victor Bentley — lay on deck. She might have been Cleopatra herself ... that imperious regent of ancient Egypt.

Victor sat at her feet. He looked thoroughly lazy and happy. His gaze never left Sandra's face. She was enchantingly lovely, lying there on her cushions, in her gauzy gown.

Here was every luxury; music, exquisite scenery. All that woman could desire for her wedding-day.

But Sandra dreaded the oncoming night. She half-regretted her marriage, she found no delight in her surroundings.

'Are you happy, Sandra?' Victor asked.

'Yes,' she said feverishly. 'Yes, I am.'

He gave a low laugh. He believed she was beginning to feel the enchantment that was holding him spell-bound.

The great sun sank like a crimson ball, and turned the green waters of the Nile to a river of scarlet. They had left the green palms behind. Now they were on the fringe of the desert.

Sunset merged into darkness, the stars came out.

Victor turned to Sandra.

She felt herself trembling. It was altogether too tremendous; the intoxication of this night and the subtle way in which Victor wooed her. Deep in her heart it was Michael ... only Michael ... and yet — and yet she was human. She wanted to forget and she believed herself this man's wife.

When he caught her close to him she did not repulse him for the space of a second. Then she felt his lips demanding against her mouth; heard him whisper:

'Sandra ... Sandra ... Kiss me!'

She revolted then. She gave a faint cry, and struggled.

'No Victor! Wait!'

But he did not care now whether she loved or hated him. He held her fast and kissed her with fierce mad kisses on her eyes, her brow, her cheeks, and her arms.

'You are mine — my wife!' he said. 'I shall never let you go again!'

But he was forced to let her go. It was not Sandra who stemmed the tide of emotion and tore herself from his arms.

An altogether unexpected outside source ended that brief night of their honeymoon.

A small boat came alongside their bigger one, which had moored for the night. Half-a-dozen Arabs in striped galabiehs climbed with noiseless agility on to the luxurious deck. They surrounded Sandra. Two brown hands dragged Victor to his feet. Livid, furious, he looked at them, his hair dishevelled, his lips snarling.

'What the deuce —' he began.

'Take the girl,' said a voice in Arabic.

Two Arabs lifted Sandra from the couch. She screamed in terror. She was being captured by the natives. It seemed too sensational to be true.

'Victor! Victor!' she cried.

But he was helpless, bound hand and foot.

She cried and struggled vainly as she was lifted without ceremony into the small boat alongside the bigger vessel. Under cover of darkness she was rowed quickly to the shore. The light on deck grew more distant. She was lifted on to a camel. A tall Arab held her and rode behind her.

At the end of half an hour's jogging, Sandra was stiff and sore, and dumb with despair. Then at last she saw lights, an oasis, some kind of encampment. There were one or two square, striped tents here, beside feathery palms. A camp-fire was burning.

The camel squatted patiently, and the Arab who had ridden with Sandra lifted her from the saddle. He carried her into the biggest tent and set her on her feet.

'Thy wishes are carried out, O Master,' he said in Arabic, to a tall Arab inside the tent. This man's face was covered. Sandra, trembling, panting, stared at him. The other man left them alone.

In the tent one oil-lamp burned dimly on a bracket. There were rugs on the ground, a camp-bed covered with cushions, some food and wine on a table beside the bed.

'Who are you?' Sandra asked the Arab desperately.

She stopped. Her heart gave a tremendous leap. A cry broke from her lips.

'You,' she gasped.

'So, Mrs. Victor Bentley,' he said sarcastically. 'We meet again. And you spend your wedding-night — with me!'

Sandra could scarcely believe her own eyes. She stared up at Michael's thin sardonic face. He shook with mocking laughter.

'A surprise for you, eh, my little bride? But never mind. One honeymoon is as good as another. A night in the desert under a million stars will be as delightful as a night on the Nile!'

'You!' said Sandra again in a choked voice, 'I never dreamed ... never imagined ...'

'I expect you wonder how I achieved this,' she heard his cool hard voice. 'It wasn't easy. But I made up my mind to get you, my dear, and I generally do what I want to. I followed you ... found out from an Arab at Bentley's villa that he had taken you up the Nile. Money was no object to me. I got the fastest car and the most reliable Arabs in Cairo. With our tents and our equipment we came along the river bank and followed the course of Bentley's boat. When you moored for the night, I sent my servants to fetch you. That's all.'

Sandra looked at him. She was as white as death; panting.

'Very clever, no doubt, Michael. But you needn't think you can behave in this outrageous fashion — that you can do what you like with me. You can't. You have no claim on me. I married Victor this morning. I am his wife.'

'Pardon me,' said Michael in an ice cold voice. 'You are mine.'

She laughed hysterically.

'Oh, no, I'm not. You treated me as though I were your property in Cairo, but you can't go on with that game. I am Victor's wife. And to him I am going back — at once.' Michael's gaze took in every detail of her appearance.

He was seething with jealous rage. The sight of her in absurd native garments infuriated him.

'Victor married me by special licence this morning,' Sandra said in a trembling voice, her great dark eyes flashing at him. 'I belong to him now. At least he did marry me; he didn't cheat me like you did, and he doesn't torture me like you do. He is kind to me.'

'Kind. For as long as you amuse him.'

'I'm not going to listen to you. I'm not going to stay here. I'm going straight back to my husband.'

She turned and moved away, but he caught her wrist.

'Your husband is here, Sandra. Not

on that boat.'

She laughed.

'Oh, no. You told me that ours was never a legal ceremony. But I was married legally enough to Victor in Cairo this morning.'

'You committed bigamy.'

She stared at him, her heart pounding. 'It isn't true!'

'It is true. You committed bigamy when you married Bentley. You are my wife, Sandra. You always have been. I told you a lie when I said you were not.'

Only for a space of a minute Sandra believed him. Then she shook her head. No — that was too absurd. He couldn't swing from one story to another just like that, to suit his own ends.

'I don't believe a word you say,' she cried. 'You are trying to force me to stay with you. You don't want me to go to my husband. But I am going to him and nothing shall prevent me.'

'I tell you he is not your husband. I am!'

'No. You are trying to defeat me. But I

91

am not going to be bullied and defeated. I know I am not your wife, and that I am his, and I am going back to him.'

Michael put his hand to his forehead. It was wet. His pulses raced, Heaven, what a fool he had been ever to tell Sandra that story. He saw that she definitely refused to believe him now. He tried to argue; to assure her, but she remained adamant. She tried to get out of the tent, away from him.

'Let me go!' she said violently struggling with him.

A wave of violent emotion swept over him. He held her closer; so close that she could feel the passionate beating of his heart.

'I shall not let you go. I tell you, Sandra, you are my real wife. I will never let you go again.'

'You liar ... you fiend!' She lost control of herself and began to sob wildly in his arms, fighting until her strength ebbed. She felt his kisses on her lips, her hair, her throat.

'You are my wife,' he breathed. 'Only

mine.'

Spent, helpless, sobbing, she ceased to fight with him. She lay against him with closed eyes, shuddering from head to foot.

Then his mood changed. He swung from fierce tyrant to tender lover. He held her as though she were a child.

'Sandra,' he said huskily. 'Sandra, my wife — my own ... you don't belong to Victor. No ... only to me, darling. Tonight is our wedding night. Sandra, won't you love me again ... forgive and forget what has passed?'

She opened her large dark eyes and gave him a look of bitter reproach that haunted him long afterwards.

'No, no ... never! You've hurt me enough — too much. You aren't sincere now. You're lying to me, acting a part. just to keep me from another man. I hate you, Michael!'

He winced. Then the thought of Victor Bentley roused anger in him again. Let her hate him. He would not send her back to that man, who had no right to her beauty and her sweetness. He bent and touched her silky curls with his lips.

'I won't let you hate me tonight, Sandra. I will make you love me again. Our second wedding ... our second honeymoon.'

After Sandra had been so roughly and rudely torn from him on their 'wedding night,' Victor Bentley was left to fume and rant helplessly. He had neither camels nor a car. He could not follow Sandra and her abductors into the desert on foot. He knew better than to do that. So he bade his men turn the boat and go back down the Nile to Cairo.

He had a pretty shrewd idea that Michael was at the bottom of this outrage. But he was not certain. The whole thing was too ridiculous.

Not once did he think of Sandra with selfless pity. He pitied himself. His bride had been taken from him. He had been cheated. That maddened him. He wanted Sandra for himself. He believed that she was legally his and he determined to get her.

He went back to Cairo, to his villa, in sullen rage to await developments. He decided that if he stayed here he would get news of Sandra; that if she managed to escape from her captors, she would make her way back here to him.

He could have gone into the desert and tried to find her, but he thought that would be both uncomfortable and dangerous. He did not wish to get shot or knifed by some Arab — even for his wife's sake. Above all things, Victor Bentley was a coward.

So he sat tight in Cairo, awaiting news of her.

Out there in the desert, Sandra was kept captive by Michael. She continued to resent him and hate him; to feel quite certain that he lied to her, that she was not his wife; and nothing he could say would convince her.

She thought a lot about Victor. And the thoughts were none too happy ones. He was a poor sort of lover and husband that made no attempt to follow and find her.

For two long weeks — days and nights of strain, of fresh humiliation and unhappiness — she stayed out there in the desert as Michael's unwilling captive. He seemed to her cruel and remorseless. Day after day, while he worked on his irrigation plans, she hung about the tents, watched by his servants, seeing no chance of escape.

Then one brilliant, sunlit morning, Sandra made her escape. The Arabs had grown used to seeing her wander about the oasis without attempting to get away. They were naturally lazy and careless. They relaxed their vigilance. Sandra watchful and still hoping to make her escape, saw that she was not being spied upon. She gave just one desperate glance over her shoulder and walked swiftly away from the oasis.

It was a foolish thing to do. She did not know her way. She had neither food nor water. But she was not responsible for her actions. Her one fevered longing was to get away from Michael ... from men and their relentless pursuit. She wanted work ... sheer, hard ... and forgetfulness.

It so happened that a caravan on its way to Cairo passed by that morning and sighted the slim, lonely figure in the filmy Egyptian dress. They were merchants from Palestine and not interested in white women, but they were kindly. When Sandra, gasping, almost in tears, stumbled over the sand toward them — already at the end of her strength after walking for an hour — they received her politely. They could not speak her language, but she kept saying 'Cairo ... Cairo ...'

So she rode on the camels with them across the desert back into Cairo.

She came back to the city a very changed creature. Haggard, desperate, unhappy, she set foot again in the city with a feeling of enormous relief that she had escaped from Michael. He was not her husband. Victor was her husband. But she did not want Victor. She remembered the fierce clasp of his arms and the insistent pressure of his lips that moonlit night of their wedding, and shivered. She had been saved from him. And now she did not wish to return to him; to submit to his arms. She wanted no lover. She had put love out of her life, she told herself.

Yet she had been mad to come back to this city, an English girl without a penny in her purse. That evening, at sundown, Sandra wandered round the streets, terrified and alone. And almost she wished she had stayed in the security of Michael's tent out in the desert. Almost there came a yearning in her for the safety of his arms and for the old, tender look in his deep grey eyes.

But she put that longing aside and determined never to see Michael again ... never to see Victor Bentley. She would, if possible, drift out of both their lives. She had been mad ever to marry Victor, just to satisfy a sense of revenge upon Michael. She turned wearily into a café in the main European quarter of the city. The café was empty except for a fat Turk with a red fez on his greasy black head with a cigar in his mouth. A pretty, tired-looking Greek woman was executing a dance in front of him. The tables and chairs were tipped up. The lights were low. The hour for the public had not yet arrived.

The Turk took the cigar from his mouth and regarded Sandra in surprise. He spoke to her in excellent English.

'Madame, can I assist you? I am Hassan Bayout, proprietor of the Thousand Stars, this estimable café.'

A thought leapt to Sandra's brain.

'Will you give me work?' she said huskily. 'I can dance.'

The Turk changed his manner. His civility gave place to a sharp, commercial manner.

'You want work ... to dance, eh? Come here. Let me look at you.'

She felt ashamed and miserable, but she obeyed him. He came close. His black eyes narrowed to slits. He made a little chuckling noise. Surely the Gods had favoured him tonight!

'Allah be praised, but certainly you may dance for me! Your name?'

'Sandra,' she said wearily.

'Sandra! Ah then you shall be Sandra, my new dancer.' He turned to the Greek woman and gave her a sharp word.

'Be off. You are no good. I don't want you.'

The woman meekly shuffled away. Sandra was sorry for her. But there was nothing to be done. One must live … and look after oneself.

The Turk questioned Sandra rapidly. She told him she had run away from home — that she was quite free, that she wished to earn her living and take respectable rooms somewhere.

Her new employer was almost childishly pleased with her.

'Tonight you shall make a name in Cairo and my patrons will shower you with coins,' he exclaimed

Sandra, drooping and exhausted, begged for rest. And then he took her to a quiet lodging-house close by, run by a respectable Turkish woman who was his cousin. Sandra was given a comfortable room where she slept soundly, worn out, until ten that night. At ten she had to dress and be at the Café of a Thousand Stars.

'Sandra, the Dancer,'was announced by Hassan Bayout as his 'new star'. She danced beautifully and achieved instantaneous success. The men cheered her wildly, roared for her to return. She was thankful, because she knew that Hassan would keep her and that she could ask a decent salary.

The days and weeks went by. Nobody discovered her hiding place. She grew accustomed to her job as Hassan's dancing-girl. The men who tried to make love to her were warded off by the Turk, whom Sandra grew to like and trust.

Then fresh disaster befell her. She began to feel ill and tired, too tired to dance with her old gaiety, and sparkle. Her lovely face grew sharp and pinched; she looked as ill as she felt. In terror she went to an English doctor in Cairo.

She emerged from his house with a fatalistic look in her great dark eyes and fear in her heart. He had told her that she was to be the mother of a child.

For the second time ... the mother of Michael's child. Without telling her employer the truth, merely giving serious illness as an excuse, Sandra left the Café of a Thousand Stars.

With curious embarrassment and anxiety in her heart, she went, that evening, to Victor Bentley's villa.

He was there. He had just returned from Alexandria. Failing to receive any news of his 'wife' he had left Cairo to make inquiries in other cities; otherwise he might have heard about the new dancer in the Café of a Thousand Stars.

He was sitting in his luxurious drawing-room; a luxurious figure himself, in a cream tropical suit, his handsome face moody.

When Sandra was shown into his presence, however, he sprang to his feet with a cry of genuine pleasure.

'You!' he said. 'You ... after all this time!'

He reached her side and pulled her into his arms. Before she could speak a word, his kisses fell on her face.

'Sandra ... my wife ... and I thought you were dead ... lost to me!' he said tensely.

His kisses did not stir her, but his joy at seeing her eased a little of the aching misery in her soul. Perhaps this man truly loved her. It would be wonderful to know that she could rely on him, now in her hour of desperate need.

Victor released her; held her at arm's length; stared at her. She was as beautiful as ever. In the dim, rich lamplight he could not see that her face was drawn and white and her eyes heavily shadowed.

'Where have you been all this time? What happened to you, Sandra? It was the most awful piece of cruelty — to have you torn from my arms on our wedding night. And what I suffered!'

She gave a faint tragic smile. It was she who had suffered most. But she said nothing. Quietly she explained.

'Victor — it was Michael who abducted me that night.'

'That man!' Victor went dark with rage. 'Listen, baby, I'll have him prosecuted, have him put in gaol, for stealing my wife!'

Sandra winced and put up a hand.

'Victor ... what does it matter, now? I have escaped. I'm back again. Victor I'm in terrible trouble. I've come to you for your help — because you are my husband. Oh, Victor, be kind to me ... be gentle with me ... for I've been through agonies.'

Her voice broke on a sob. She put her hands on his shoulders and looked up at him with swimming tragic eyes. He looked down at her in sudden alarm.

'What do you mean, Sandra,' he said. 'What 'terrible trouble' are you in?'

She flushed hotly and avoided his gaze.

'Victor, I — I am going to have a child!'

'Good heavens!' he exclaimed. He moved back from her. 'You — my wife — going to have a child! And it isn't mine. It can't be. Is it his — Michael's? Go on ... answer me ... is it?'

She said:

'Yes,' in a low, trembling voice, and hid her face in her hands.

When Sandra looked up — trembling violently — she was aghast to find herself looking into the face of a fiend rather than a man. There was no tender pity in the eyes of Victor Bentley — no kindliness, no compassion for this young mother-to-be. Only a fury which convulsed him.

'So, that's it!' he said between clenched teeth. 'That's it! You are going to have a child. And it's his — Michael's! You lived with him out there in the desert. You gave him your kisses. And then you come to me!'

She shrank back, panting, white to the lips.

'Victor — listen — be merciful — be reasonable. Michael abducted me — took me from you by force. I wasn't willing. Oh, you know it!'

'Not willing, eh? That may be. But you are to bear his child, and you are my wife! A pretty thought.'

She gave a little moan and hid her face again.

His eyes blazed hatred at her. He no longer wanted her. He no longer considered her fascinating.

'Get out of here." he said in a brutal voice.

Horrified, she looked at him.

'But Victor ... I'm your wife ...'

'You are, but I'll divorce you. You can go to Michael. He took my wife; now let him keep her.'

She turned and stumbled from the room; walked with pitiful, unsteady footsteps out of the luxurious villa into the hot, starry night.

She could not think, could not decide where to go or what to do. She only knew that nothing — nothing — nothing on this earth, would induce her to go to Michael to risk being sneered at and cast off by him. One man's brutality had been enough tonight. She would never go to him. She must live alone; work for herself and her baby. Her poor, unhappy, ill-fated child.

She was exhausted after the terrible scene she had been through with Victor. She was in no fit state to stand it. She had been feeling ill when she went to the villa to the man she called 'husband'. Now she felt ready to die.

She came to the main street where she was jostled by a crowd. She felt her head spinning, limbs aching. She wondered how long she could go on walking. Not very long. . . . She collapsed beside the wide marble steps of a big European hotel. A place with a wide veranda on which there were many small tables, with rose-coloured lamps, and men and women in evening dress dining, because it was cooler out here than in the hotel.

Two people saw Sandra's slim figure sway and fall. Two people rushed to her aid. A woman and a tall good-looking man with twinkling blue eyes.

'Say, mother,' the man exclaimed with a Southern American drawl. 'The little girl's fainted. Come on and have a look at her.'

'Why, I surely will!' said the woman,

and putting a wrap around her shoulders, hurried down the hotel steps. A black commissionaire was bending over Sandra, but the two Americans waved him away. The commissionaire touched his cap and retreated. The lady was a very well known woman doctor in New York, Dr. Mary Vanfelt. And the son, Beverley Vanfelt, was equally well known as a writer in America.

Dr. Mary Vanfelt lifted Sandra's head on to her lap and looked down at the lovely, tragic young face.

'Why, isn't she just the most beautiful thing, Beverley!' she said.

'I've never seen a face so wonderful!' he said with enthusiasm. 'And she looks a mere child. Is she bad?'

'No. It's only a faint. She looks kind of exhausted. What'll we do with her?'

'A hospital, I suppose,' said Beverley Vanfelt in a regretful voice.

'Why, no. She shall be taken up to my sitting-room first,' said Dr. Mary in a firm voice. 'I've kind of taken a fancy to this child's face. I want a talk with her.

Look, Bev — she's coming to!'

Sandra opened her eyes. She looked dazedly up into two faces — the kindly jolly one of a grey-haired lady, the clear-cut, equally cheerful one of a tall, thin young man.

'Oh!' she whispered. 'Where am I?'

'You're all right,' said Dr. Vanfelt. 'Just try to get on your feet. I'm going to take you into the hotel. You're English, aren't you, my dear?'

'Yes,' said Sandra dazedly.

She managed to stand up. The woman took one arm, the young man took the other. And Beverley Vanfelt was distinctly thrilled at that contact.

Sandra, like one in a dream, came thoroughly to her senses in the beautiful and luxurious private sitting-room of Dr. Mary Vanfelt. Beverley was told to come up later. Dr. Vanfelt made Sandra lie on the sofa against many soft cushions. She made her drink hot coffee and eat some sandwiches. And then, when she saw the faint pink colour steal back to the death-white cheeks, she allowed Sandra to talk.

'I've kind of taken a fancy to you, honey,' she said. Sandra had never known a woman with so charming and happy a face and manner, and it warmed her unhappy, lonely young heart. 'Just tell me everything. I guess I'm your friend right now.'

So Sandra told Dr. Vanfelt everything.

Mary Vanfelt sat beside her and listened to her amazing story. Sandra told it simply, but without mentioning any names, save her own Christian one.

When she had finished, the older woman said:

'Why, say, it's more complicated and romantic than anything my son Beverley has ever written in all his born days. What a very amazing thing! My dear, I'm thankful you fainted right outside my hotel.'

'Why?' asked Sandra with a faint smile.

'Because I'm going to look after you right now.'

'But why should you?' asked Sandra astonished. 'I'm a complete stranger to you and —'

'But I like you,' said the lady doctor warmly. 'And I adore babies. That's my work in the U.S.A. I've been sent to Egypt for a rest. I've got to stay here for a long time; and Beverley, my son, is staying with me — writing a book. Now, I'd just adore having an interest like this. You've been cruelly treated by these men, you poor child. Will you place yourself in my hands and let me see after you?'

Sandra broke down. She broke down and wept. Great aching sobs shook her from head to foot. This was too much kindness, and it overwhelmed her. She had been through such hours of mental strain. The future had appalled and terrified her. Dr Vanfelt let her cry and held on tightly to one hand. Then she said:

'Now calm down, honey, and remember that baby. You've not got to upset yourself over all this. I'm going to ring the bell and order a bedroom for you close to mine, and you're going straight to bed, Sandra ... I shall call you that. But what else are we going to call you?'

'Oh — Mrs. — Smith,' Sandra decided

111

in a low voice. 'I don't feel I want to call myself by — my real name.'

'Sure, then it'll be little Mrs. Smith. Not that it goes well with Sandra,' said Mary Vanfelt with her jolly laugh. 'And, understand, honey, you're in my care, and these men are right out of it. You don't want to see either of them again, do you?'

A second's hesitation. So far as Victor was concerned Sandra wiped him out instantly — loathed and despised him. But she could not quite eradicate Michael from her mind and heart so easily. She had worshipped him so. And it was his child which she would bear in the days to come. But he didn't love her. Better, far, never to see him again.

'No — I don't want to see — either of them,' she said in a low voice. But the tears ran down her cheeks, and Dr. Mary Vanfelt, being a woman, was quick to realise that Sandra had loved the father of her child and, in her broken, unhappy heart, still cared for him.

9

During the months that followed, Sandra stayed in the Hotel Oriental with the Americans and was completely adopted by them. She had vanished, so far as Victor and Michael were concerned. And since that night when she had told Dr. Vanfelt her tragic story, she never mentioned either of the men again.

Mary Vanfelt was wonderfully kind to her. Befriended her, mothered her, doctored her all in one. And Beverley Vanfelt, when he learned that the beautiful Sandra was an expectant mother, was kindness itself, and could not have been more gentle or attentive if he had been her brother.

They moved from the hotel finally and took a villa where it was quieter. It was in that villa that Sandra's daughter was born. Michael's daughter. Not the son of her imagination. But a tiny, rather frail girl with her mother's great dark eyes. In every other respect she was the image of her father.

Sandra did not know whether to be glad or sorry. It brought back all the heartbreak and grief of the old lost love, yet at the same time she resented the resemblance. It made her feel fiercely maternal and possessive.

Michael might want his daughter if he saw her. He must never see her — never! Sandra, the young mother, adored her baby, and she would never give her up to a living soul.

Those were happy days, in a measure, in the quiet, beautiful villa which stood in an enchanted garden. Mary Vanfelt, friend and doctor, was always with her. Beverley, writing his new book, was not so wrapped in work that he could not afford the time to see a good deal of Sandra. It was he who drove her and the baby out in his car for her first drive and for many others after. He who read to her; talked to her when Mary Vanfelt was busy or out. And, as was inevitable, he fell very desperately in love with Sandra.

After the birth of her baby, she was ten times lovelier than she had been before. The hollows in her face and throat filled out. A look of peace replaced the misery of her great dark eyes. There was an added sweetness in her voice, her manner. Beverley Vanfelt often looked at her and listened to her and thought what a wonderful lover she must have been, and how much he would like to make her love him now. But he said nothing to her yet. It was too soon.

Sandra was immensely grateful to her friends, and liked and trusted Beverley Vanfelt. But she was heart and soul wrapped up in her tiny daughter, who had been christened 'Mary Sandra' — Mary, after Dr. Vanfelt, who was her godmother. And Mary Sandra was a good baby, who rarely cried, and more often than not smiled adorably into her mother's beautiful eyes.

As time went on the baby thrived and grew stronger. She also grew more strikingly like Michael. And that always caused Sandra a pang.

When little Mary was three months old, Beverley Vanfelt asked Sandra to marry him.

'My dear, I'm just crazy about you,' he told her, with his soft, Southern drawl. 'I don't care what happened in your past. I just want to pick you up in my arms and hug you and take you right back to New York as my wife. Mother's got to go back next month. Say, honey — darling — will you get a divorce from this man in Cairo, whoever he is, and marry me?'

Sandra did not know how to answer him. She sat beside him, that sunlit afternoon in the gardens of the villa, a slim, beautiful figure in a gay cotton sun-bathing dress.

She looked eighteen rather than the mother of a child. Beverley Vanfelt adored her. And she liked him. He was a charming, lovable man. Yet she knew she could never love him as she had Michael, with fierce passion, with all her heart and soul. She told him so.

Beverley kissed her hands, each in

turn.

'I'll have to risk that, honey. If you'll marry me I'll be good to you. In time, maybe, you'll care for me. And I'll be the best father in the world to Mary Sandra.'

Sandra's eyes filled with tears. She wondered if it would not be best to let this kind man who loved her take her and her baby to America. She could wipe out the past completely then. Oh, Michael! Why couldn't she forget?

It was agreed between them that she should try to secure her divorce from Victor Bentley. She promised to leave her baby with Dr. Vanfelt, and visit Bentley that very afternoon.

'Hurry back, honey,' Beverley told her, 'There's a fellow whose work I'm interested in dining with us tonight and I want him to meet you.'

Sandra promised to hurry back.

With Beverley's kisses on her hands and nothing in her heart for him but gratitude, she left the villa and took a hired car to Victor's home.

The moment she was within the

grounds of that wonderful place — it seemed evil now, in its exotic splendour — she felt miserable and afraid. But she was determined to go through with her mission. Yes, she would get a divorce from Victor. He would be glad to give it.

She announced herself to the Arab who opened the door to her. He returned almost at once to tell her that the master would see her.

Sandra after a period of ten long months faced Victor Bentley again.

He was once more the sauve, indolent man she had first known, not the brutal creature who had flung her out. But she despised him when she saw him. He looked at her in astonishment. Heavens, how lovely she had grown he thought. Being a mother suited little Sandra. Her beauty was ripe, glowing, more than ever intriguing.

'So you want a divorce, do you, my charming wife,' he drawled.

'Yes,' said Sandra curtly. 'Please arrange it at once.'

He narrowed his gaze. He came closer

to her, and put a hand on her shoulder. She drew away.

'Don't touch me, please!'

'Oh, so you're feeling peevish?'

'Peevish!' she repeated with a scornful laugh. 'That doesn't describe it, Victor. I hate and despise you!'

'Ah!' he bowed. 'That's trying. I've made up my mind; I'm not going to give you a divorce.'

'What?'

'No. I'm going to keep my wife. She is too beautiful and attractive to hand over to some other man. You have had his child. You say you have left her with friends. Let the friends keep her. But I am going to keep you!'

Sandra gasped and tried to elude his arms. But they closed about her like a vice. All the old terror consumed her. The colour left her face, the peace fled from her eyes. She was the old Sandra, pursued, hunted. She gave a low cry.

'Let me go; Victor — let me go! I won't stay!'

'Oh, yes you will. You'll have to stay. I

shall keep you with me ... my wife!'

She felt his lips brush her mouth. Panic seized her. Why, why had she come alone? Why hadn't she brought Beverley Vanfelt? She had never dreamed Victor would want to keep her, would behave like this. She thought frantically of the peace of the Vanfelts' home, of her little daughter, whom she adored. She struggled desperately in Victor's arms, screaming:

'Let me go — let me go!'

There was consternation in the Vanfelts' villa that night when ten o'clock came and Sandra had not come home.

Sandra's little girl, the only one unconscious of disaster, slept peacefully in her cot. But Mary Vanfelt was worried to death, and Beverley was like a man distraught.

'If only I'd insisted on going with her!' he kept on saying. 'But she seemed so confident she'd be all right. And I don't know where she's gone. I don't know the name of this man she's married to.'

'I suppose it isn't possible she meant

to go — meant to stay away —' said Mary Vanfelt, in a low, unhappy voice.

'Why mother, what a terrible thing to say!'

'I know. I feel ashamed. And yet, what can be keeping her out all this time? And Bev, we must admit we knew nothing about her when we took her in.'

Beverley Vanfelt went very white. 'If you're insinuating Sandra —'

'Oh hush, my dear,' said his mother. 'Don't let's be rash or jump to any conclusions. Let us wait and hope.'

'Meanwhile we have a very distinguished guest. We had better tell him what our worry is,' said Beverley.

'Yes. He seems such a nice man,' said Dr. Vanfelt.

They rejoined their guest of the evening. A big handsome man with grey eyes that were peculiarly sad, and a lined, bitter face.

He could see that his host and hostess were harassed and troubled, and he wondered what was wrong. They explained. He looked at them curiously.

'It sounds a most intriguing story. You say this girl fainted outside the Hotel Oriental? What was her name?'

'She called herself Mrs. Smith,' said Dr. Vanfelt. 'So lovely; the most magnificent great dark eyes.'

'Yes, poor Sandra," said Beverley.

The guest of the evening started violently. He went white under his tan, and astonished Vanfelt by seizing his arm with a grip that hurt.

'What?' he exclaimed. 'Sandra ... did you say?'

'Yes,' said the American staring. 'Do you know her, Mr. Hunt?'

Michael — who had come here tonight to give Beverley Vanfelt an account of irrigation works in the desert — put a hand to his head.

'Yes ... if it is the same ... and it must be. I know her. Your story is my story. Sandra ... married me in England, and I am the man who took her from Victor Bentley's boat on the Nile.'

'You!' exclaimed Vanfelt. 'Good God! Then I reckon if I'd known you were that man I'd never have asked you here tonight.'

'Why?' demanded Michael, breathing rapidly.

'Because you were a brute — a fiend to her — you drove her almost to suicide.'

'Wait,' said Michael, 'what do you know of the details of this case? There is my side also.'

'Sure, that's fair,' said Mary Vanfelt, who, woman-like, found something very attractive in Michael's hard, brown face and steely grey eyes.

'Sandra was not quite the little saint she made herself out to be,' said Michael. 'God knows, I loved her — adored her when I married her. Then I found out what she was, what she had done. Shall I tell you my sister's tragedy — how her husband, Lancaster, shot himself through Sandra? Sandra, the model whose name rang throughout England. A case you Americans would not have known. But everyone else knows.'

Beverley sank into a chair.

'Say, is that true?' he said in a low voice. 'Can what my mother thought be right . . . that lovely girl is an adventuress?'

'She may have deserted that dear little baby right now,' said Mary Vanfelt sadly.

Michael's handsome head shot up.

He made a rapid mental calculation. His face flushed. Yes ... that baby must be his. Unknown to him, Sandra had borne him a child ... a daughter, after she left the desert.

He looked at Dr. Vanfelt.

'Will you take me to see the child?' he asked.

'Sure,' she said. 'If you wish.'

She led the way upstairs to the room which was now a spotless white nursery for Sandra's child.

Michael saw in a rose-coloured crib a child of three months, fast asleep. And he had only to bend over and take one look to know that this was indeed his daughter ... his own flesh and blood. The likeness to himself in that baby face was remarkable.

He went down on one knee beside the cot and took one of the baby's fists between both his big hands. In that hour all the hardness was wiped from his face. Mary Vanfelt, watching him saw the tender, affectionate man under the mask.

'My baby,' he said in a hushed voice. 'My little girl. What is her name?'

'Mary, after me ... Sandra, after her mother.'

Michael's brow contracted. Her mother. Oh, how he had loved her mother!

'It is such a tragedy that the little one has no right to your name,' murmured Dr. Vanfelt.

Michael stood up. His face was flushed.

'Dr. Vanfelt — you can take my word for it that my daughter has every right to my name,' he said proudly. 'Sandra is my wife. Her marriage to Bentley was illegal — bigamous — although she did not realise it. And anyhow I am going to ask you to give me permission to take my daughter to her rightful home — with me.'

'But Sandra —' began the American.

'Isn't it obvious that Sandra has deserted her baby — just as she deserted me in the desert?'

'I suppose so,' said the woman perplexedly. 'Sure, it's real hard for me to know what to do.'

'Let us leave it like this,' suggested Michael. 'If Sandra does not return in another twenty-four hours, you will know that she has gone willingly, and for good. Then I will come for my child.'

'Very well,' said Mrs. Vanfelt. 'I guess we'll leave it at that.'

But Beverley Vanfelt was not content.

He demanded Victor Bentley's address.

'If Sandra doesn't come home tomorrow, I shall go and find out what happened,' he said. 'I cared for her. I guess I ought to see if she's all right.'

The subtle rebuke in that stirred Michael to say:

'You are right. Sandra is my wife and mother of my child. I'll come with you Vanfelt.'

The two men sat up all night talking. There was no going to bed for either of them. And morning came and still Sandra had not returned.

Then they went together to Victor Bentley's villa, the other side of Cairo.

They found it shut up, deserted, silent as the grave. There was no trace of Sandra ... or of Victor Bentley. Michael and Beverley faced each other — both conscious of bitter disappointment. Michael said:

'It is as I thought. Sandra never meant to return. Now, if you allow me to, Vanfelt, I will take my child away. Sandra will never see either of us again.'

During the long night, whilst Michael Hunt and Beverley Vanfelt sat up waiting for Sandra to come back, Sandra herself had passed through hours of bitter, passionate struggle with Victor Bentley.

Nothing that she could say or do would persuade Victor to let her go this time.

'No, my charming wife,' he said again

and again. 'You're much too attractive. You're ten times more beautiful than you used to be. You shall stay with me — your husband — and we will forget everything that has been before.'

His lips brushed her burning cheeks, touched her lips, pressed them in a fierce kiss. No man had kissed her for so long, she felt horror-stricken. And she felt, very definitely, that since she was the mother of Michael's child, Michael would be the last man who would ever hold her or kiss her. Their love was ended. But at least it was also the end of love, all passion — for her.

She struggled frantically in Victor's arms.

'Let me go! You must! You shan't keep me here! Victor, don't you realise that Beverley Vanfelt will be here in a minute. I told him to fetch me — gave this address!'

She told the lie desperately, in terror. Victor Bentley released her for a second. He looked at her under frowning brows. If that were true, he didn't want any Americans messing round his villa. He suddenly decided that it would be wiser altogether if he took Sandra away from Cairo — out of reach of her new friends. Swiftly he contemplated flight in his boat. He had been about to go up the Nile for a pleasure trip. It was waiting for him, ready to move off at any minute. The difficulty would be to get Sandra aboard.

He had a subtle, cunning brain. It did not take him long to make plans and act upon them. He assumed an expression of remorse.

'Sandra, my dear, I'm sorry. I've been a brute to you. Forgive me. Your aloofness drove me mad I'm afraid.'

Much relieved she stood there, watching him, her great dark eyes still pitifully frightened.

'Victor — then you'll be decent — you'll let me go?'

'If you must.'

'Oh thank you,' she said brokenly. 'Yes, please — please do. I don't want a lover — believe me. I only want my baby.'

Victor crossed the room and pressed a bell.

'Before I open the door to you, you shall drink some coffee with me ... show me you are friendly,' he said.

'I'd rather go at once.'

'No — just for a few moments! After all — you are my wife. And if I am going to have the ceremony anulled, you might as well have a few friendly moments with me to remember, Sandra.'

She gave in.

'Oh, very well. Just a little coffee,' she said.

She was very tired and in need of a stimulant. And not for an instant did she imagine that there would be any trickery, that Victor was acting a part. It just seemed to her that he had repented and decided to be decent and let her go.

Victor Bentley ordered that coffee, speaking to his head servant in a tongue Sandra did not know. She did not, therefore, realise, that he also ordered a certain potent sleeping draught to be put in the cup which was to be handed to her.

She drank the sweet, hot black coffee unsuspiciously and enjoyed it. She looked at Victor with more friendly eyes.

'I'm glad you understand — how much my little girl means to me, Victor,' she said huskily.

The drug worked rapidly. Almost before Sandra realised it, she was unconscious. It was just as though the sumptuous room faded queerly away ... She no longer heard Victor's voice or saw his smiling face. She fell across the cushions on the divan and lay helpless, insensible.

Victor picked her up in his arms.

'Now, my lovely one,' he muttered. 'Our honeymoon begins again ... and this time you shall learn to love me.' Within an incredibly short time, the beautiful villa had been emptied of its inhabitants and was shut up — deserted — silent as the grave, which was how Michael and Beverley discovered it at dawn.

Long before dawn, Sandra's unconscious form was carried on to Victor's boat. She was laid under the awning on a couch to sleep off the effects of the drug.

When morning broke, they had drifted many miles from Cairo down the jade-green river. Sandra recovered from that drugged sleep, opened her heavy eyes, and found herself moving along on the sunlit waters. She realised then, how wickedly she had been tricked.

She sat up on the divan, pushing the curly hair back from her face. She managed to stand up, gasping, filled with nameless terrors. She was quite alone. Victor, who had been up all night, was asleep in the interior of the boat. An Arab who had been posted to watch his master's wife had gone in search of a cigarette — believing the lady to be still safely asleep.

Sandra staggered to the rail. She saw, opposite her, the palm-fringed shore. She did not know in the least where she was.

She looked down at the green waters of the Nile glittering in the brilliant sunshine. She was a fine swimmer and she decided to use her powers of swimming now. Nobody was watching.

Sandra stood for a moment, poised gracefully in her sun-bathing dress. She dived cleanly into the river. Just a faint splash and she was gone. The boat moved on without her. The shock of the cool water against her thoroughly roused her. She was strong — even exalted — when she made her way with swift strokes to the shore. She climbed out of the river and stood awhile in the blazing sun which dried her glowing face, she ran — ran like one pursued — through a group of palm trees — further inland, where neither Victor nor his men would discover her.

It was the evening of the same day when Sandra reached Cairo. She had had a difficult time getting back to the city. But she got there, and the mystified and furious Victor, when he discovered she had vanished, thought that she had flung herself into the river and drowned herself.

But Sandra — very much alive — was

taken by a passing caravan back to the city.

She went back to the Vanfelts' villa. Her one desire was to see her baby. But there she met with a shock. The Vanfelts, her kind friends, had gone, and her baby had gone with them. Aghast, Sandra questioned a caretaker. The woman, eyeing her queerly, informed her that Mr. Vanfelt and the lady doctor had left for America that morning.

'But my baby — the little girl,' gasped Sandra.

'The baby went with an English gentleman,' she was told.

The caretaker could not tell her the name, but she had seen the Englishman and described him. Sandra's heart almost stopped beating while she listened. For she knew beyoud doubt that it was Michael. He had found his daughter ... taken her away!

Sandra reviewed the situation in terror and dismay. She was not going to let Michael keep her baby from her. Oh, this was what she had feared, right from the beginning!

She made her way from the deserted villa to Michael's old flat in Cairo. She prayed, sick with fear, that she would find him there — find her baby daughter there, too. Like a panic-stricken creature, she rushed past an anguished Arab who opened the door of the flat to her — crying:

'Michael! Michael!'

It was all so familiar, this flat, this place which had once been her home. She flung open the door of the sitting room. And then she almost burst into tears with relief. She saw the tall, well-remembered figure of the man she had once adored and who was the father of her child.

The same Michael . . . the same thin, brown face and stern lips; pipe in hand; grey eyes staring at her amazedly.

'You — Sandra!' he exclaimed.

'Yes,' she panted. 'I've come for my baby. You've got my baby here.'

His face changed. He stiffened.

'Yes, that is quite true. My daughter is here,' he said.

His daughter. How possessively he said it! The young mother clenched her hands convulsively.

'My baby — oh, so much more than yours!' she said passionately. 'I worked for her ... have had her all these months. You're not going to take her away from me now.'

'You deserted her,' said Michael coldly.

'That's a lie,' she said in a frenzied voice. 'I adore my baby — I would never desert her.'

'Then why did you leave her and never return to the Vanfelts?'

'What do you know about it? How did you find my baby?'

'I happened by a strange coincidence, to be Beverley Vanfelt's guest at dinner on the night you were missing. They told me your story and showed me the child. l knew she was mine.'

'I see,' said Sandra in a hollow voice.

She sank heavily into a chair and hid her face in her hands.

'I'm absolutely done,' she whispered.

Michael saw that she was in a state

of exhaustion and nerves. He ordered a brandy for her.

'No — my baby — I want to see her,' she said.

He looked at the bowed curly head of his wife. His heart was pounding. The sight of her, after this long time, stirred him more than he cared to admit. And she was, after all, mother of his child. He had to remember that.

'Before the child comes, will you please give me some explanation of these last months, Sandra,' at length he said.

In a low voice she told him everything that had happened.

'You had no right to keep the birth of my daughter from me,' he said.

'Why not? You had treated me cruelly … broken me to bits. I never wanted to see you again.'

'So you went back to Bentley,' he said grimly.

'To ask for my release. I hated and loathed the thought that I was married to him and that Mary Sandra was —'

'Console yourself on that point,'

137

he broke in, in a cold voice. 'You were never married to Bentley. Our marriage — yours and mine — was legal enough. Hunt is the child's rightful name, and this is her home.'

Sandra stared at him, her heart pounding.

'You mean that? Oh, what am I to believe? You lied to me ... deceived me ...'

'I admit it. To punish you, I lied. I regret it now, and you are hearing the real truth. You are my wife — not his.'

Sandra stared at him — her whole soul in her eyes. He looked back at her sternly — without flinching. She knew that this time he did not lie. Immense relief flooded her.

'Thank God!' she said in a heartening voice.

His brown face reddened. He felt ashamed, in that moment. And somehow this Sandra — so tired and broken, and tragic touched him. And how could he deny that he was strangely, fiercely glad to see her again? Love for her was far from dead in his heart. But she gave him no chance to say a kind word. She was on her feet now, quivering, furious.

'The agony you have caused me over my baby — the outrage of it!' she choked. 'And I thought I was Victor Bentley's wife ... loathing him ... terrified of him ...'

Hot words stumbled out ... lashed him. A bitter and graphic description of last night's terror ... how she had been drugged and carried on to the boat. It was impossible for Michael to do otherwise than believe her, to deem her innocent, at least, of abandoning her child.

But he could not yet forget his sister — or Hugh Lancaster.

'Now that you have come back, you must stay with me. You are my wife and mother of my baby,' he said, using the same hard, chilling voice. 'Shortly I shall be resigning from my post in Egypt and we will go back to England.'

The door opened. A tall girl in a white pique dress entered, carrying a baby in a short white gown. In a second Sandra was holding the baby in her arms, hugging it, crooning over it.

'My baby . . . my darling . . . my little one,' she whispered, her tears, falling thick and fast.'

Michael, hands in pockets, stared at her under frowning brows. He was moved and did not want to be moved. He had no desire to give way to emotions which he believed were better stamped on ... killed.

The nurse glanced at him. She was an English girl whom he had engaged this morning, in Cairo. She had a handsome face, large brilliant eyes and very fair — almost golden — hair, not cut short, but braided about her head. She was the antithesis of Sandra, who was so little and slim and dark. She had come with an excellent reference, and Michael thought her a splendid nurse. She, on her side, secretly a passionate, headstrong woman, had already fallen desperately in love with the grey-eyed, thin-lipped man whom she had thought a widower. It was a considerable blow to her to find that he had a wife alive who had come back to him. Such a pretty wife, too.

Sandra handed the child back to her.

'Take her,' she whispered, struggling with her tears. 'And be very, very careful with her. Has she all her things here?'

'Yes,' said the nurse. Then added coldly: 'From whom do I take my orders?'

'From Mrs. Hunt, of course,' put in Michael awkwardly.

'Yes, Mr. Hunt,' said the nurse, her tone much softer and left the room.

Sandra looked up at Michael.

'We are agreed, then, that I stay with you as your wife and Mary's mother. But otherwise ... there can be no friendship or understanding between us.'

Michael inclined his head.

'Quite.'

'Then if you will excuse me, I will go and change these clothes. My trunks, I presume, were sent here from the Vanfelts'

'Yes.'

'And Beverley Vanfelt, who asked me

to marry him, has returned to America, thinking the worst of me,' she said bitterly.

'I shall write and tell him you were not guilty that night — but a victim of Bentley's,' said Michael.

'Thank you,' she said with sarcasm. 'And I had also better write Victor Bentley and inform him that my marriage with him was bigamous and that he can consider it annulled.'

'That it so.'

'It is an outrage and should never have happened.'

'None of it would have happened if you had not behaved as you did in Lancaster's lifetime,' said Michael.

She winced.

'So you still harbour the old mistakes against me? You are malicious and hateful,' she flashed. 'I shall stay with you only on account of our child. But I'd prefer never to see you again.'

She swept out of the room. Michael put his pipe in his mouth. His pulses were jerking. Malicious and hateful!

That's what she thought of him. Perhaps she had cause.

But she had made him so. Once he had adored her, trusted her ...

There commenced from that time onward a period of great unhappiness between these two who misunderstood each other. They saw each other at meal times, in the evenings. Otherwise, they were as strangers. Michael did not even visit his baby daughter unless Sandra was absent from the nursery.

Nurse Mitchell became a bone of contention between them. She was always sweet and tactful with Michael — careful to please him. She was as frigid and disagreeable to Sandra as she dared to be.

Sandra was quick to see that the girl was in love with Michael — and she bitterly resented it.

One evening when Michael came back to the flat from work, he found a flushed, stormy-eyed Sandra waiting for him.

'I have told Dorothy Mitchell to leave tomorrow,' she said.

143

'Good heavens — why,' demanded Michael.

'She is in love with you.' said Sandra.

Michael flushed — then laughed.

'How ridiculous.'

'It's true, I tell you. I entered the nursery this afternoon to find her mooning over your photograph, which I had hung in the room for Mary.'

Michael laughed again.

'Rubbish!'

'I tell you it is true. She is in love with you. She is a sly creature, and always rude to me, and I will not have her with my baby!' flashed Sandra.

Michael stared down at her. And suddenly realised that she was jealous, yes — jealous of Dorothy Mitchell. He did not give a second thought to the young nurse. She was quite pretty — but she did not appeal that way to him. But now he knew that Sandra was jealous, it struck him that he might make use of the fact. How often in her life she had made men jealous . . . broken their hearts — his amongst them. Let her feel a little of that unbearable pain.

'I forbid you to force that girl to leave our service,' he said calmly. 'She is a good nurse to Mary, and she shall stay.'

'Very well,' said Sandra breathing hard. 'If she stays— I go. You can choose between us.'

'You are being childish and unreasonable,' said Michael. 'I don't believe a word of this business about the girl being in love with me. Mooning over my photo! — what rubbish, Sandra.'

'I tell you I saw her — with my own eyes!' said Sandra hotly. 'It is insulting for me for you to take her part — to keep her here when I wish her to go!'

Michael's own temper blazed.

'I tell you the girl is a splendid nurse for Mary, and she shall not be turned out just to satisfy a distorted, uncalled-for jealousy!' he exclaimed.

For a moment Sandra was on the verge of turning on her heel and marching out of the flat. Then her rage subsided. She grew ice-cold. A weariness, a sense of hopeless misery — almost of despair —

crept over her. What, after all, was the use of this discussion? What good was she doing by this exhibition of anger and jealousy? If she were jealous of this attractive golden-haired nurse, she was lowering her pride horribly by showing it. And she was not jealous, she told herself. Why should she be? If Michael had an affair with Dorothy Mitchell ... with a dozen other women ... why should she be jealous? It didn't matter to her.

Unhappily she looked up at her husband's stern hard face, and the feeling of despair intensified. She knew that it did matter ... that she could not endure the thought of another woman in Michael's arms.

But she gave in.

'Very well,' she said in a low voice. 'Let the nurse stay.'

Michael frowned. Then he, too, climbed down.

'Of course, Sandra — you will admit she is a good nurse?'

'Yes,' she said.

'Well — if there is any truth in this

absurd business about her being — er — in love with me she must go. But let us keep her another week on trial. Good English nurses are hard to get in Cairo.'

'Very well,' said Sandra in the same tired, flat voice. Michael lit a cigarette. He felt suddenly embarrassed. It was all very awkward, anyhow.

Sandra rang, and told the insolent-faced Nurse Mitchell, when she answered, to bring the baby in. Yes, Nurse Mitchell was good with baby. Sandra's love for her baby filled her heart. She could not help but think: 'Michael loves his child'

That was curiously pleasing to her. She wanted him to love his child. Hers — as well!

Outside the door Nurse Mitchell had been standing during the discussion between husband and wife. Her pink-and-white face was distorted with rage, her hands trembling. She had heard every word.

'So Madame guesses I'm in love with her husband, and wants to throw me out, does she!' Dorothy Mitchell thought. 'Well — if anyoue goes from this home — it won't be me!'

She opened the door boldly and entered. She handed Sandra the baby. Sandra gave her a long, searching look. But the nurse's white lids drooped. She gave nothing away. The moment Sandra's dark head bent over the baby's downy one, however, Dorothy Mitchell raised her eyes to Michael's face. She sighed, and a passionate look came across her face. She was frantically in love with this big, grey-eyed stern Englishman. And she was determined to attract him somehow. She was pretty well certain that he was not on amiable or lover-like terms with his wife.

Michael hastened from the room. The presence of the nurse made him thoroughly awkward now. He did not even look at her.

That night, when baby Mary was asleep, Nurse Mitchell sat down and wrote a letter. It took her a lot of time and trouble. And between every line she looked up at the photograph of Michael Hunt which hung on the nursery wall over baby's white cot.

Her pulses thrilled when she looked at it. She was madly in love.

She was out to get Michael — somehow. She was without balance over love affairs. Her only good point was her capability so far as babies were concerned. Curiously enough, she was a good, conscientious nurse.

10

Next morning, when Michael had gone to his office, Dorothy Mitchell stole into the dining-room and placed the letter which she had written on the desk, on top of the blotter. She was standing there, looking at it, when she heard Sandra enter. She gave a cry — half simulated, half genuine — of fright, and hurried from the room.

Sandra, tired and depressed after a broken night, stared after the girl's retreating figure and frowned. How scared she had looked. What was she doing at that desk? Then Sandra walked across the room and saw the letter lying on the blotter.

She would not have dreamed of reading a letter written by Nurse Mitchell; but in this case she had to read it. For she saw the beginning ... in letters of fire the words danced before her.

'Michael, dear...'

Sandra's whole body filled with rage, with jealousy. 'Michael, dear ...'! How dared Dorothy Mitchell write to Michael in that familiar, intimate style? So that was what she was doing ... writing a letter to Michael. That was what she, Sandra, had interrupted!

With trembling fingers Sandra lifted the letter and read the rest of it:

Michael, dear,

It was sweet of you to snatch those few minutes with me last night. I know things are difficult ... but don't despair ... our love will triumph. Oh, darling, I look forward to our next meeting. All last night I was dreaming about you ... Michael ... Hotel Imperial de Desert ... don't forget ...

There it ended, as though the writer had broken off abruptly.

Sandra's indignation and anger knew no bounds when she finished reading that letter. Every word of it bit into her imagination — like acid. It left no room for doubt. Michael was having an affair

151

with the nurse. Last night, when he had denied it, laughed about it, he had lied.

He was a hypocrite. He had snatched a few moments to say goodnight to the girl. They were on such terms that she called him 'Michael, dear,' and 'my darling'. And they were having a meeting, some time or other, at the Hotel Imperial de Desert. That was an isolated and famous place some twenty miles out in the desert from Cairo, mostly frequented by tourists and very romantic and beautiful. Sandra had heard of it.

Just for a few moments she was tempted to rush into the nursery, face Dorothy Mitchell with this letter and accuse her, order her to leave the flat. Then her first wild fury died down. She would not speak to this girl who was so mean, so unscrupulous as to have an affair with another woman's husband. No, thought Sandra, she would never speak to the girl again. But tonight when Michael came home from work, he should see this letter, and it should be he who would dismiss Dorothy

Mitchell; he who should turn her out. And if he refused, then she — Sandra — would go.

Sandra would have gone at once, now ... if it had not been for Mary Sandra. But for the baby's innocent sake she decided to stay. It was not right to rob the child of her father. She should not suffer. Michael must turn this girl out, forget his affair with her.

Sandra walked into her bedroom. She sat down on the edge of the bed, her slim, nervous fingers playing with the note that had — she thought — enlightened her as to the real position between Michael and the nurse. A terrible feeling of desolation came over her. Michael ... and that girl!

Sandra flung herself face downwards on her bed, and suddenly the tears rained down her cheeks. She choked with sobs. Her body shook with a tempest of grief. For nothing ... neither time, nor cruelty, nor injured pride could totally erase her love for this man who had been her only lover in every sense of the word, and was father of her child.

She managed to compose herself at length and waited for her meeting with Michael when he returned from work ... waited for the storm which must inevitably break over them when she showed Michael the letter.

She bathed and changed her dress and emerged from her room. She clapped her hands for Selim. She did not wish to see Dorothy Mitchell. She was going to ask Selim to tell the nurse she need not bring baby to her this afternoon. Selim told her, however, that the nurse had not yet returned from their afternoon walk.

This astonished Sandra. Baby was always in by four-thirty. It was now half-past five. What was the girl doing? She was a little anxious: She went out on to the balcony. The sun still streamed down. It was hot and close outside. There were ominously dark clouds coming up from the direction of the desert ... marring the flawless cobalt blue of the sky. A storm was brewing.

Sandra stood on that balcony, watching, waiting, for an hour. At half-past six the blue sky was decidedly grey and the sun had gone in. The atmosphere was stiflingly hot, surcharged with electricity. A terrific storm was about to break over Cairo. And the nurse and baby were still out. What could have happened.

Sandra was filled with sudden frantic fear. She rushed to the telephone and called up Michael's office.

A young Frenchman, who was Michael's head clerk, answered:

'Monsieur left half an hour ago,' he said.

'But he hasn't reached home!' exclaimed Sandra.

'No, madame, he went to the desert,' said the clerk.

Sandra put a hand to her throat. A little pulse beat there thickly:

'To the desert? On business?' she asked.

'I do not know, Madame. He received a wire and left immediately for the desert,' said the clerk politely.

Sandra hung up the receiver. She

put a hand to her head. It burned and throbbed. Michael had received a wire and had gone to the desert. Where? Why? Was it to the Hotel Imperial de Desert ... to meet that girl ...? And was baby Mary Sandra with them? Was he base enough to include his tiny daughter in his amorous tryst? Sandra was like a mad creature. White, burning-eyed, trembling, she paced up and down the flat, wondering what to do; panic-stricken — first of all about the baby — then about Michael's infidelity.

The storm broke over Cairo. Great raindrops like hailstones beat against the windows. Through the hot, stifling air came the thunder-claps — harsh, reverberating peals, one on top of another. Across the dark heavens the fork lightning flashed brilliantly. Zig-zagging blinding light.

Tropical storms always worried Sandra, strung up her nervous system. This evening she was like one demented. She lay on her sofa, her fingers pressed to her ears so that she could not hear the awful thunder crashes, her eyes hidden. And she asked herself again and again frantically:

'Where is baby ... where is Michael ... where is that nurse?'

At six o'clock that same evening, Dorothy Mitchell was settled very comfortably in a bedroom in the Hotel Imperial de Desert, and Mary Sandra — much too young to know where she was, and quite happy because she was cosy and comfy in a nice cool bed — was sound asleep, also in the Hotel Imperial de Desert.

Dorothy Mitchell had left the pram at the station in Cairo and hired a car to bring her and Mary here. Having got there, she had sent a wire to Michael at his office; an urgent wire which said:

Come to Hotel Imperial de Desert at once. Mary Sandra here. Something terrible happened.

She left it unsigned, and left Michael to put his own construction on it.

157

She was playing a dangerous game, but she was a desperate woman — man-mad — driven by the most passionate love for Michael. She knew the wire would bring Michael here without delay, and once she got him here — then she would play her part for all she was worth. She had signed the register 'Mrs. Hunt.' That seemed a good beginning.

It was a most beautiful and luxurious hotel, run by a French syndicate; as magnificent as any hotel in Paris. Great white terraces facing the wonderful expanses of the Sahara; a garden full of palms; of exotic flowers; Arab or Greek servants in spotless white linen robes; every bedroom palatial, fitted with every modern luxury. It appealed to Dorothy Mitchell. And still more did it appeal to her that this place was absolutely isolated — twenty miles from Cairo.

Then the great storm broke. Baby Mary awakened and grew fretful. Dorothy Mitchell hated storms and became very nervous and anxious. The darkness and driving rain blotted out the beautiful scenery. She was intensely relieved to hear a car drive up to the hotel. She ran out in the rain on to her balcony and peered down. The lights from the hotel entrance shone on the tall figure of Michael. So he had come — alone. Thank heaven!

Feverishly, Dorothy unpinned the golden braids of her hair, and began to tear her neat uniform dress a little from one white shoulder. She shivered with excitement. When Michael rushed into the room — not knowing what or whom to expect — he saw the nurse standing there — looking dishevelled — and exceedingly pretty with a mass of golden wavy hair tumbling to her waist ... and her face drenched in tears.

'What's happened — where is baby — where is my wife?' were Michael's first words.

Dorothy Mitchell stumbled towards him.

'Oh, thank heaven you've come.'

'What is it? What's happened?' He stared at her. Then he saw the baby in the bed and his face lit up. 'Mary is there — all right — thank God for that!'

'It's been terrible!' moaned Dorothy Mitchell. She swayed towards him. 'I'm exhausted ...'

Confused and perplexed, Michael put out his arm to support her. She immediately fell against him. He was embarrassed beyoud words. Her trembling form, leaning against him; her tumbled hair, her flushed, wet face, made him feel most awkward.

'My dear girl — what has happened?' he asked almost crossly.

Then Dorothy burst out with the story she had planned. Weeping bitterly, she described graphically the 'terrible time she had had'. How she had brought baby for a walk in the park in Cairo, and been attacked by two native thugs. These men had carried her and baby off, driven them in a car to the desert, robbed her of a little ring and locket she wore and of her purse; even taken a tiny gold chain bracelet from the darling baby's tiny wrist.

'It's a wonder worse didn't happen to me with those horrible men, but I fought, I bit ... I scratched ... and I defended baby,' Dorothy said hysterically. 'Oh, Mr. Hunt, I wasn't afraid for myself, but I was terrified for the darling baby. I would have defended her with my life.'

Michael listened, amazed and horrified. The poor girl! What a ghastly experience for her! But thank God, little Mary Sandra was all right. His precious daughter. Michael looked with eyes full of love at the tiny, rosebud face of his child. Then he looked with gratitude at the nurse. She had fought nobly to defend the baby. In the hands of thugs ... poor girl ... no wonder she was overwrought and hysterical.

'I'm immensely grateful to you for what you did,' he said. 'Tell me, how did you get away?'

'They were disturbed ... by a passing caravan ... and ran off and left us ... and we struggled here, to this hotel, where I immediately wired for you. I didn't tell Mrs. Hunt — I thought it would be such a shock to her.'

'Quite right,' said Michael.

She made pretence of gathering the torn pieces of her uniform dress together, but not before Michael had seen the pretty, white throat which had been exposed, and recognised for the first time what a pretty woman she was — what marvellous golden hair she had.

'Those devils didn't — didn't —?' he began, confused. She lowered her lashes prettily.

'One horrible Arab tried to — kiss me — to threaten to hurt baby if I didn't let him,' she stammered. 'I was prepared to do anything — rather than have baby hurt.'

That seemed to Michael most touching, and he was deeply moved. What a fine, noble girl . . . prepared to sacrifice so much ... rather than have the baby hurt. He held out his hand.

'With all my heart I thank you,' he said.

She swayed nearer him. A violent crash of thunder shook the hotel. The storm broke out with renewed violence. Dorothy clung to Michael, shuddering. He thought she was still thoroughly unnerved by her terrible experience and tried to comfort her, gripped her hand. She smiled with her face hidden in his shoulder. She had gained a triumph. And, of course, it never for an instant entered Michael's head that every word Dorothy had spoken was — from beginning to end — a lie.

He left her and went downstairs to telephone Sandra. She would be dreadfully worried about the child, and she must know how bravely Nurse Mitchell had behaved. He was perturbed to find that the big storm had put the telephone out of action. He was even more perturbed to find the car which had brought him to the desert hotel could not take them back. Something had gone wrong with the engine, also due to the storm. There was no possible way for them to get back to Cairo that night.

Michael was thoroughly put out and nettled. But he had no choice.

He went up to the nnrse's room.

'I'm afraid we're stuck here for the night,' he said with a worried frown.

Her heart leaped, but she answered demurely:

'Oh — but how — awkward!'

'You and baby will be all right in here,' he said. 'I'll get a room and we'll have to turn in — just as we are — without luggage. I can't get a call through to Mrs. Hunt — the wires are down. And the car's out of action. But the chauffeur thinks he can get it mended by morning, and we'll go back as early as we can.'

For the rest of that evening Michael was anxious and restless. He did not like being here in this isolated hotel with Dorothy Mitchell. And there was a look in Dorothy's blue eyes that Michael found most disturbing. It alarmed him. He admired the girl for what she had done today; but he did not like the expression in her eyes. It rather proved that what Sandra had thought was right. Dorothy Mitchell was in love with him.

When he said goodnight to her outside

her bedroom door, she lifted her face, as though for a kiss. He barely looked at her, turned and marched into his own room.

Dorothy Mitchell's spirits fell. Sulky, furious, she entered her room and closed the door. What was the man made of — stone? He didn't love his wife. Why couldn't he see that she, Dorothy, was offering him her love? Surely the invitation in her eyes just now had been made plain!

Neither of them slept that night. Michael walked up and down the bedroom, smoking innumerable cigarettes, worrying about Sandra ... it was strange, but he wanted Sandra tonight. Wished desperately that she were here ... that he could go to her; clasp her in his arms and say: 'Beloved, I still love you ... let us forget the past and be lovers again.'

He scarcely gave a thought to Dorothy Mitchell. But she lay awake all night, weeping in thwarted longing, all the more determined to get him.

The night and the storm passed. Dawn

broke — serene — exquisite — rose and pearl over the misty face of the Sahara. And when the sun rose higher, and was shining brilliantly over Egypt. Michael was strangely exalted. He was going to ask Sandra to begin again.

He rushed into the flat calling her name eagerly:

'Sandra! Sandra!'

She emerged slowly from the sitting-room. Her appearance gave Michael a shock. She was pale, and her great dark eyes were violet 'shadowed. She was like a frozen statue, however, cold as ice, bitter.

'Michael,' said Sandra. 'You have spent the night at the Hotel Imperial de Desert — with that girl. And you were base enough to take baby — our baby — with you during your disgraceful intrigue. You are pretty brazen. You are worse than Victor Bentley — than any man I know!'

'My dear Sandra — are you mad?' he said hotly. 'You don't know what you are saying.'

166

'Do you deny you spent the night at that hotel?'

'No. I know I did. I tried to phone you, and the wires were down in the storm. I did stay at the hotel ... but not with Nurse Mitchell, which is what you insinuate.'

'I don't insinuate — I state a fact,' said Sandra, still ice-cold, deadly in her calm. 'You had an assignation with her there, and the excuse of the storm enabled you to remain the night.'

'That's a lie!' exclaimed Michael, red to the roots of his crisp brown hair.

'It's the truth!' she said with her hands clenched. 'Yet you denied that that girl was in love with you — or you with her.'

'I deny it now.'

'Then what about this ... which I found on your desk after lunch yesterday?'

Sandra thrust the letter which Dorothy had written into her husband's hand. Michael read it. He was aghast. He looked up.

'The girl must be mad ... Every word

is an untruth!' he cried hotly. 'Good heavens!'

'Then what were you both doing at that hotel?'

Michael broke into a passionate explanation repeated Dorothy's story of the native thugs who had attacked her; of his rush to save her and the baby. Sandra only laughed.

'You fool, Michael — do you think a poor story like that convinces me? No. This letter gives you away.'

'Look here, Sandra — every word is untrue and the whole thing is a concoction.'

'No, Michael. You are having an affair with Dorothy Mitchell and last night was a put-up job between you. I despise you both!'

Michael's grey eyes blazed.

'I won't stand for this!' he said. 'Nurse Mitchell herself shall come in and tell you the story of her terrible struggle with those chaps and tell you there is no love between us.'

Before Sandra could speak, the door

168

opened. Dorothy Mitchell walked slowly in. She was pale and trembling, and her golden head drooped. Sandra looked at her in horror and disgust.

'What have you come for?' she demanded.

Dorothy lifted her head and gave Michael a look of intense longing.

'I want you to ... to know the truth, Mrs. Hunt,' she faltered.

'Quite right,' said Michael. 'Tell her thr truth, please.'

'Very well,' said Dorothy.

'Mrs. Hunt, you ought to know. I love your husband, and he — he is my lover! We stayed as Mr. and Mrs. Hunt at the Hotel Imperial de Desert last night.'

Michael stood like one dumbfounded. The treachery, the base intrigue behind Dorothy Mitchell's declaration rendered him speechless for a moment. It had never entered his head that she could so lie, or wish to separate him from his wife. And although her liking for him had been evident at the desert hotel, he had supposed it to be an idle infatuation and not for an instant imagined that she was serious.

Now she deliberately gave Sandra the impression that they had stayed at the hotel as man and wife. The unspeakable wickedness of it — and from this golden-haired demure-looking girl! Who would have believed it?

Dorothy Mitchell eyed him from under her lashes. She was whit and nervous. She had done a very dangerous thing and she was not yet certain what the consequences would be. It was to her that Sandra first spoke.

'Leave this room — leave my flat — at once. Don't dare touch my baby again!' she said in a low passionate voice.

Then Michael's wrath burst into flame. Shaking, white under his tan, he said:

'Sandra — you don't believe that? It's a lie, I tell you! There isn't a grain of truth in what she says!'

Sandra turned to him eyes narrowed.

'There is no truth in what you say. I do believe her. The thing's obvious. You stayed together last night in that hotel. All this business about a telegram from her to say she was attacked by thugs is a thin story which I don't believe. I'm not an absolute fool. You have behaved most disgracefully. You, Miss Mitchell, leave this flat at once. And you, Michael, hadn't you better follow her?'

Michael gasped with sheer rage.

'But you're crazy to believe her, Sandra. She's a liar, I tell you, and I swear to you that we did not stay together.'

'And in what name did you register?' asked Sandra coldly.

Michael, breathing hard, reflected a moment, swallowed as though something choked him.

'I — I didn't register at all.'

Dorothy saw her chance here, and took it.

'Oh, Michael!' she said softly. 'You did. It's in the book ...'

'It's a lie,' he broke in, his eyes flashing at her. 'How can you have the impudence, the audacity, to stand there and tell my wife such frightful lies?'

Dorothy began to cry.

'If Mrs. Hunt doesn't believe me … perhaps she'll ring up the hotel and find out … she'll see for herself.'

'I shall find out,' said Sandra coldly. 'Wait.'

She walked to the telephone, waiving aside her husband who began to protest against the insult of this. She took up the receiver.

'The wires are in order again,' she said, her great eyes fixed upon Michael. 'I can get the Imperial. Just wait …'

'It's an outrage … the whole thing!' exclaimed Michael.

Sandra was speaking now to the reception clerk at the Hotel de Desert.

'A lady and a gentleman with an infant stayed at your hotel last night,' she said. 'Would you kindly tell me how they registered?'

The clerk answered in the space of a minute.

'They registered as Mr. and Mrs. Hunt, madam.'

Sandra, her cheeks scorching, turned

to Michael. With a slender, trembling hand, she held out the receiver to him.

'Ask for yourself,' she said.

Michael seized the telephone.

'What names did you say registered at your hotel last night?' he demanded.

'Mr. and Mrs. Hunt, of Cairo sir,' came the somewhat surprised response. 'But why —'

Michael hung up and cut off the inquisitive voice. He, too, was red with shame. He looked at Dorothy Mitchell.

'So you did that, too, did you? Good God, there isn't much you've left undone.'

Dorothy broke into loud weeping.

'Oh, Michael ... fancy letting me down like this. Fancy putting all the blame on me! How cowardly!'

'Yes, you are a coward as well as a blackguard,' said Sandra bitterly. 'I'd think more of you if you came straight to me with the honest truth.'

'But it is the truth,' he exclaimed. 'Look here, Sandra, I swear by ...'

'Oh, don't!' she broke in. 'The evidence is good enough for me, and I've thought all along that there was an intrigue between you and this girl.'

'What can I say to persuade you that she is lying?' he asked in a voice of impassioned despair.

'Nothing,' she said coldly, and walked past him to the door.

'Where are you going?'

'To my room — to pack. Baby Mary and I will go. You and your . . . your lover . . . had better stay here. You won't want us.'

'Sandra!'

He tried to stop her, but she walked swiftly from the room and slammed the door.

He gasped and turned to Nurse Mitchell. She was sobbing into her handkerchief.

'May I ask what you hope to gain by doing this disgraceful and wicked thing?' he demanded furiously.

She shrank away.

'Michael — don't be angry. I ...'

'Angry!' He almost shouted the word.

'I could kill you for this. How dared you stand there and lie so blatantly, so despicably, to my wife, knowing that you would separate us? And you faked the whole thing, did you? Brought me out to that place because I thought my little girl was in danger. You faked it ... shammed. All right, Dorothy Mitchell, we shall see what you gain by this business.'

She looked at him with eyes grown suddenly terrified. She threw herself against him and locked her arms about his neck.

'I love you ... I did it because I loved you. Forgive me ... don't send me away. Oh, please be kind.'

'You were not so kind when you told my wife things that will come between us for ever,' he broke in sternly. He unloosened her arms and pushed her away from him. 'I have no pity for you.'

'I love you — I swear it.'

'Love doesn't allow one to do such terrible things. Go and pack and get out of here.'

'No ... No!' She fell at his knees and

clutched his arm. Her face was white and smeared with tears. 'I love you. Don't send me away.'

He gave her a look of scorn, of anger.

'Get up and leave this home. You've done enough harm,' he said.

She ran out of the room, crying hysterically.

Not until she had gone and the Arabs had followed with her luggage, did he attempt to see Sandra. Then sick at heart, loathing the whole situation, he went to his wife's bedroom. He knew she had locked herself in there — had been there with the baby since the nurse had left.

He knocked on her door.

'Sandra, let me in.'

'No,' said her voice ... a hard, bitter young voice. 'Go to Dorothy Mitchell.'

'Dorothy Mitchell has gone. I have turned her out of the flat. The whole thing was a fabrication, an attempt on her part to separate us,' he said impatiently.

'I refuse to believe that.'

'Don't be mad, Sandra. I'm telling you the truth. Why else have I sent the woman away?'

'Perhaps you want to spare yourself a divorce,' came her reply ... 'But you won't. I intend to divorce you at once.'

'Good heavens, Sandra ... but listen ...'

'Nothing will make me change my mind. You can keep to Dorothy Mitchell ... or any other woman you like. I shall not live with you, and baby shall not live under the roof of such a father.'

Michael lost his patience.

'Sandra, I won't stand much more from you. Open that door.'

'No.'

'Open it, or by heaven, I'll break it in.'

'Mary is asleep. By all means burst in and frighten her to death. You've done her enough harm already, taking her away for the night with you on such an escapade.'

Michael, white to the lips, marched away from the door. He was certainly not going to frighten Mary. But a veritable passion of anger, of resentment, consumed him. How dared Sandra speak to him like that? It was cruel and wrong of her to condemn him so utterly. So she meant to divorce him! And who was she to judge, to condemn, after her affair with Lancaster ... her conduct since?

He was so angry that he did not pause to see that it was jealousy which prompted Sandra's ready acceptance of the worst. He thought that this was malice on her part — that she was trying to get back on him. And the longer he brooded over the affair the more certain he became that he had been a fool to think kindly of her; to want to begin again; to soften his heart. His longing for her remained ... but the gentleness, the tenderness behind it, vanished.

She had threatened to divorce him ... to separate him from his little daughter who he had grown to adore! But no, he would show her she couldn't do that. Later, he would show her ... prove to her that he was still master.

11

Sandra refused to emerge from her bedroom until late that afternoon when the golden, eastern day was waning and the dark shadows of night were falling over Cairo.

Restless, brooding, Michael waited for her to come out. He had made up his mind that he would not be disbelieved and dictated to by Sandra.

She knew he was waiting, and in some curious way she dreaded facing him. But she had to come in the end. She had no lunch or tea, and she could not remain indefinitely in her room. She must get her luggage carried down from the flat and find a car and some lodgings for herself and the baby. It was too late to get away now, so she would see Michael since he insisted upon it, and make him understand quite definitely that tomorrow she would leave him for good and all.

She was met by him in the cool wide corridor of their spacious flat as she emerged from her room. He gave one quick look at her travelling coat and hat.

'Sandra, what is all this nonsense? You can't mean to leave me.'

'But I do,' she said. Her heart began to pound as she looked up into his grey, furious eyes.

'At this time of day?'

'No,' she broke in. 'I shall go tomorrow morning. I regret it, but I shall have to stay another night under your roof.'

'Sandra, I have sworn that the nurse ...'

'Please don't waste your breath,' she interrupted him again. 'I know you are guilty. I have had quite sufficient evidence ... enough to satisfy a judge, at any rate, that I am entitled to divorce you.'

'Very well ...' he laughed, but it was a terrible laugh and his control was snapping. Sandra felt her heart miss a beat as she looked up at his furious face. Those grey, handsome eyes were blazing. 'Very well. You shall go — tomorrow. But tonight you stay with me. You are still my wife, Sandra ... still my wife — do you understand?'

She did understand. A scarlet wave of colour spread over her lovely face and throat. She drew back.

'No ... No ...' she stammered.

'Yes,' he said, and caught her and held her in a remorseless embrace. 'You are still my wife and shall not forget it. For months ... for a whole year ... you have forgotten. A year in which you cheated me. You believe the worst of me. You think me rotten, faithless? Very well, Sandra, you shall see me live up to the reputation you give me.'

Her breathing quickened so that it seemed to choke her.

'Oh, no ... no,' she said again, in a whisper. 'Michael. for heaven's sake.'

He laughed and picked her up in his arms.

'A whole year,' he whispered. 'And you are sweeter than ever ... your lips have the old allure ... Sandra ...'

Early the next morning Sandra was up and dressed before Michael was awake. She left him in his room and went to her own room to dress Mary Sandra, and prepare her for departure from her home. She gave one last look at her husband's handsome form as she tiptoed from the room.

She was white, almost grim, as though the emotional storm which had broken over her head last night had stunned her. And she knew that those hours when she had been held in the arms of this man could never be wiped out or forgotten. But she told herself she was finished with him for ever, never wanted to see him again.

How still he lay! Curiously young and handsome with his dark ruffled hair, and a hand under one brown cheek. The bitterness, the cruelty of his lips had softened. He seemed to smile in his sleep.

She thought of his pitiless kisses; punishment of his remorseless passion for her and she shivered and turned from him.

'Goodbye, and this time for always,' she whispered as she left him.

A fortnight later Sandra and her little girl had settled down to a new life in a furnished room in Heliopolis, run by a French woman, and both clean and respectable even though humble. It was a very different life from the one of luxury, of almost exotic beauty which she had lived in Michael's beautiful flat. It was difficult to have to save every penny and deny herself every luxury. But she preferred it to accepting another halfpenny from the man whom she believed had so grossly betrayed her.

Sandra was working again. The kindly Turk who ran the Café of a Thousand Stars — Hassan Bayout — was only too willing and eager to re-engage 'Sandra the Dancer' who had been such a huge success a year ago. She was lovelier than she had ever been. He immediately gave her a contract. She earned sufficient to support herself and the child. And she denied herself most things in order that the little one should have every luxury that Michael could, himself, have given her.

She started divorce proceedings, citing Nurse Mitchell as co-respondent and giving evidence from the Hotel Imperial de Desert. But even while she did this thing, she was tortured. This man was the only one in the world for whom she had ever cared, no matter how deeply he had wronged or failed her. She could never get that fact out of her head. It was torment to cut the last binding cord between them ... sever their marriage tie and give him to another woman. But she did not hesitate.

And then one day she received a letter from Victor Bentley. A letter half tender, half sarcastic.

I was truly glad to hear that you committed bigamy when you married me, my elusive wife. It has saved me a lot of trouble. Consider our marriage cancelled. I will see that the annulment goes through. I am now going to Spain to meet a beautiful lady whose dark eyes remind me of yours and who is kindly disposed towards me. So farewell, my Cleopatra ... I shall never forget the sweetness of your kisses. I hope your very immaculate husband will satisfy you. —V.B.

Her very immaculate husband! Sandra tore the letter in half and was angry to find herself in tears. Why should she cry ... because of a few words from Victor Bentley? Because he hoped she would be satisfied ... and oh, how dissatisfied she was. How unutterably miserable.

She felt an aching, blinding pain in her heart when she went to the Café of a Thousand Stars that night.

The Café was full of foreigners, of Arabs and Turks and Americans, was blue with smoke from cigarettes and cheroots. Glasses clinked. There was a babel of voices and laughter. Fifty pairs of amorous eyes fastened upon the slender, graceful figure of Sandra, the Dancer: exquisite, utterly alluring in her golden dancing frock ... Sandra, whose eyes were brilliant under their dark, thick lashes ... whose lips were forced into a smile, while her very heart was breaking.

Michael came down to the Café that night. And if his own heart was breaking nobody would have guessed it. His face was hard, his lips were stern and cynical. He talked to nobody, and his moody eyes never left Sandra. How he hated her obstinacy which made her go on with the divorce. Probably she would get it. And it was hideously unfair. He had hardly set eyes on the wretched girl who had caused all the trouble.

He smoked and drank and watched her and his eyes held the look of a man tortured.

A young Greek who had been making signals to Sandra the whole evening and been ignored, got up when the last dance ended, stepped into the middle of the floor and caught her arm.

'Dance with me,' he said roughly. His eyes frightened her. 'Dance with me ...'

'No ... leave me alone,' she said, shrinking back.

A crash. Somebody's glass went over

as Michael leapt to his feet and pushed his table aside. He came to Sandra's side. He put his lithe form between the Greek and herself.

'Get out of here,' he said furiously.

Sandra put a hand to a heart that was pounding. So he was here ... he had been watching her. Strange! She was glad to see him ... to have his protection ... and yet she was divorcing him in a few months' time!

The Greek flew into a violent rage and drew a wicked-looking knife from the folds of the sash round his waist. Michael was looking at Sandra and did not see it, but she saw it.

She screamed.

'Michael ... look out ...'

She was too late. The Greek, mad with anger at the Englishman's interference, plunged the knife into Michael's side.

Michael gave a sharp cry and his knees sagged. A mist veiled Sandra's beautiful, frightened face from him. Then he crumpled up on the ground and lay there very still.

Sandra stared down at Michael's fallen body. For a moment the smoke-thickened café seemed to spin around her. She thought she was going to faint. Then a crowd of men rushing from all sides of the room obliterated Michael from her.

The Greek who had stabbed Michael had dropped the knife on to the floor. He stood dramatically still, arms crossed on his chest, his face livid. His expression was one of defiance. His bright, dark eyes remained fixed on Sandra the dancer, for whom he had committed this crime. He made no attempt to get away.

Then Sandra gave a long, wailing cry: 'Michael . . . oh, Michael!'

She pushed her way through the crowd surrounding the fallen man. She struck out fiercely with her clenched fists when somebody tried to bar her way. She fell on her knees beside Michael. She thought he was dead. He lay so still, his face was marble-white and his eyes were closed. From a wound in his side the blood was welling. For all she knew, a fatal, mortal wound. And she knew, too, that she loved him better than anyoue or anything on earth. Despite all their differences of opinion, their violent battles of will, their recent separation, she loved him. She thought he was dead, and it was more than she could bear

'Oh, Michael!' she cried agonisedly. 'Oh, Michael, my dear! ...'

She burst into passionate heartbroken sobbing. She crouched beside him, pillowing his head on her lap. She smoothed the thick, crisp hair back from his forehead.

The little crowd round the injured man fell back. Hassan Bayout was pushing his way forward, his fat face a study in anger and dismay. It was not often that such things happened in his café. The Thousand Stars was a respectable place. It would do his name no good in Cairo if it came to the public ear that an Englishman had been stabbed by a young madman of a Greek. And all over Sandra ... the beautiful dancer.

'Zut, zut, get out of the way!' he growled, elbowing his way through the noisy, garrulous crowd. 'Let the Englishman have air. Here is a doctor. An Americaine.'

He tapped Sandra's white shoulder. She looked up. Her lovely face was convulsed with grief. She looked like a beautiful broken toy, in her glittering draperies, with the flashing jewels in her disordered hair.

'Who is the Englishman, Sandra?' he asked.

She answered in a heart rending voice:

'He is Michael Hunt — my husband.'

Hassan Bayout flung up his hands in dismay.

Two local policemen had entered the café by this time. The would-be murderer, still glaring defiantly round him and muttering words of passionate pleading to Sandra, who took not the slightest notice of him, was arrested and conveyed from the café.

The American doctor (who had been watching the dancer and having coffee and a cigar in the famous café) went down on one knee beside Michael. He made a swift examination, then called for towels, which were brought to him. He hastily bound up the wound.

Sandra — her face chalk-white — her slim body trembling — wanted to ask him a question and dared not. The American saw what lay in her eyes — the most glorious eyes he had ever seen in any woman's face. He spoke to her kindly:

'Don't look so scared. Is this your boy-friend? He's all right. He's not dead.'

The colour came back to her cheeks. She breathed more naturally. She said in a broken voice:

'Oh ... then is he ... will he live?'

'Why, sure, I hope so. The knife that Greek stuck in him missed a vital part by half an inch. But that's good enough. He's all right.'

'Oh, thank God,' said Sandra. And she added in a low voice: 'He is my husband.'

'Oh,' said the doctor under his breath. And wondered why the English wife of snch a well-dressed, good-looking Englishman should be dancing for her living in an Egyptian café.

'Is he — can he be taken to his own flat?' asked Sandra.

'I reckon so,' said the doctor, bending over Michael again. 'He'll want a bit of nursing and care.'

'I can do it,' said Sandra at once.

She forgot that she was divorcing him, that she lived in lodgings apart from him, She even forgot the existence of Mary Sandra for a moment. She could only look down at Michael ... at his pale face and ruffled hair which made him look so young, so helpless.... At the blood-stained towels with which the doctor had staunched the wound ... and remember that once she had loved him with all her heart and soul.

The doctor succeeded in stemming the flow of blood.

'Now I just want to get him home and get him properly bandaged up,' he said, turning to Sandra. 'I'll drive you both to wherever you live and nip back to my own place for my bag.'

192

Someone had given Sandra a cushion. She put it under Michael's head, then left him and rushed to change from her flimsy iridescent dancing-dress to her ordinary clothes. While she was putting on her shoes she suddenly remembered that she had no right to go to Michael's flat and nurse him. Baby Mary was waiting for her at her lodgings in Heliopolis.

She put a hand to her head. She felt it whirling. Of course, she ought to go back to her baby. She must go back. But first she must make sure that Michael was all right. He mattered to her still so terribly! And if he should die! ... It would be awful — horrible — for him to die in the prime of life and through her. Yes, it was through trying to save her from the insults of a Greek that he had been stabbed tonight in the Café of a Thousand Stars.

She hastily scribbled a note to Madame, who kept the rooms in which she now lived. She asked her to keep an eye on baby until she was able to return, and explained that owing to an accident she might not get back until dawn. It was very late now, and in a very short while the glittering eastern night would merge into the glowing tints of a new day.

12

Michael was lifted and placed in the care of the American — Dr. Paige. Sandra pillowed his head on her lap. When they put him on the seat, he moaned and opened his eyes. He whispered one name:

'Sandra ...'

Sandra felt her whole heart go out to that faint call. She took one of his limp, nerveless hands and pressed it tightly. She smoothed his forehead, which was hot and damp. She whispered back:

'Michael ...!'

But he did not hear. He had drifted into unconsciousness again.

They reached the building which was so familiar to her; the big white house with its verandah and balconies; its garden full of beautiful palms and flowers. The upper flat belonged to Michael. Once it had been her home. She was shivering with a kind of nervous excitement when they got to the front door and Selim, Michael's head servant, let them into the flat. Selim's liquid eyes expressed horror when he saw the two Arabs carry in the prostrate figure of his master.

'Allah, but is the master dead?' he exclaimed.

'We hope not, Selim,' said Sandra.

He looked at her curiously. He was wondering why the beautiful wife of his master had ever left this home and what she was doing here now, so mysteriously, when his master had said that he no longer had a wife.

Michael was carried into his bedroom.

Sandra ordered the boys to bring hot water and prepared to help Dr. Paige dress Michael's wound.

'You aren't afraid?' he asked her, as he took off his coat, rolled up his sleeves, and washed his hands.

'No,' she said quietly. 'Anything you tell me to do, I'll do.'

'That's great.'

Sandra said:

'Oh — look— he' s coming to!'

Michael stirred and moved on his pillows. A groan came from him. At once the doctor moved to his side.

'We don't want him to be conscious while this dressing is being done. Just an injection, Mrs.—'

'Mrs. Hunt,' she said.

'That's right — thanks.'

Michael returned to his senses and to a sudden realisation of pain which reduced him to insensibility again.

Dr. Paige worked deftly and silently.

In the drawing-room, while these two worked to repair the damage that had been done to Michael — a tall, fair girl, in a grey flannel suit and grey felt hat, had been restlessly pacing up and down.

She had been here an hour, waiting to see Michael. And when he had been carried in, wounded and insensible, she had made herself scarce, but listened intently through a chink in the door and learned what was going on. She knew now that he was hurt. But the reason for it all remained a mystery.

One thing, however, was clear to Dorothy Mitchell. Michael's wife had come back to him. That drove her mad. She had not seen Michael since he had turned her out of the flat. All her efforts to win had failed. She knew she had failed utterly in every way, but one. And in that she had succeeded. She had separated him from his wife. So she refused to give up hope.

She had come here tonight and boldly walked into the flat. She had told Selim she intended to wait for Mr. Hunt to return home. Selim, in his anxiety over the attempted murder of his beloved master, had forgotten to mention this fact to Sandra.

Dorothy Mitchell weighed things up in her mind and came to the conclusion that there was still a fighting chance for her. If Michael were unconscious — all the better. He wouldn't be able to deny anything that she said. But she must make a last, desperate effort — for she was penniless and unable to find work without a reference. She was ready with a fresh pack of glib lies, therefore, when Sandra finally opened the drawing-room door, walked in, and found her there.

Sandra stopped dead on the threshold when she saw Dorothy Mitchell. She flushed hotly, and her heart sank. Dorothy Mitchell here ... that girl!

Sandra had left her husband's bedroom relieved beyond measure by the knowledge that he was not going to die. In fact he was a long way from it. The wound was now dressed and the patient quite comfortable. Michael was not yet conscious. The doctor was confident that he would have a good night, and recover rapidly.

'He has a magnificent constitution. I should imagine,' Dr. Paige told Sandra.

And with those encouraging words he went away. So, no-one had seen Sandra go on her knees beside the bed and kiss one of the unconscious man's hands ... cover it with burning, passionate kisses ... and whisper:

'Oh, Michael ... darling ... thank God!'

She walked into the drawing-room asking herself whether she would not be a crazy little idiot to go on with this divorce. She loved Michael ... loved him still — desperately. She could not cut away from him finally, could not bear life apart from him a day longer. He must care for her too; otherwise he would not have bothered to protect her in the café tonight.

And he had come there to watch over her ... that seemed pathetic and wonderful. He regretted that mad night in the desert with Nurse Mitchell. It was her, Sandra, he loved. Yes, she would stop the divorce proceedings and they would begin again — for baby Mary's sake as well as their own.

It was with these passionate thoughts that Sandra walked into the room and found Dorothy Mitchell. The shock was intense. The girl was there behaving as though the place belonged to her; coat and hat off; lying on a sofa, smoking a cigarette.

'What are you doing here?' Sandra asked in a voice of ice, although her whole body vibrated with anger; with bitter resentment.

Dorothy Mitchell simulated astonishment and rose slowly to her feet, taking the cigarette from her lips.

'Might I ask the same question of you?'

'How dare you —' began Sandra.

'One moment,' interrupted Dorothy Mitchell boldly. 'I understood that you and Michael had separated and were being divorced.'

Sandra winced.

'Michael swore to me that he had not seen you since the day you left my service.'

'Then he's a liar,' said Dorothy calmly. 'He sees me every day of his life ... and most evenings. I came here tonight because he asked me to. I was waiting for him to come home. Why are you here. Does he know?'

Sandra shut her eyes. For an instant blinding pain and disappointment consumed her. It was such a ghastly blow to find that Michael had lied again, that he saw this girl every day, and that she had come here tonight to see him at his request. And why should she,

Sandra, disbelieve it?

So that was the end of her dream of reconciliation. That was the end of — everything. Let Michael continue to see Dorothy Mitchell and entertain her at midnight in his flat. Perhaps one day he would marry her — when he was free.

'He shall have his freedom,' Sandra thought bitterly now she regretted those kisses, those tears, wasted on him tonight — the anguish, the devotion, the prayers for his recovery!

She pulled herself together and turned from Nurse Mitchell's malignant smile.

'Mr. Hunt — was hurt in a café tonight, and he has been brought home and put to bed,' she said in a low dull voice. 'I helped the doctor — Dr. Paige. He will come again in the morning. I am going now. You are quite right. I — have no right here. I'll leave him — to you!'

She walked quickly out of the flat. Dorothy's glittering blue glance followed, and her sinful heart leapt in triumph.

So the last desperate effort had succeeded — so far. Sandra had gone. And now to deal with Michael. Not so easy. But, under the circumstances ... with a few more lies ... a little more skill ... it might be achieved.

Sandra passed slowly and very wearily out of her husband's flat. There was a stricken look in her eyes. She was leaving him — to that girl!

Why must she go on loving ... loving a man who gave her no happiness, but only this torture ... this unbearable pain!

Michael opened his eyes in the early hours of the morning to find himself in his own bed, with a stiff, painful feeling in his side, and his body swathed in bandages. For a moment he was dazed; he could not remember what had happened, Then it an flashed back. The café, the beautiful, graceful figure of Sandra in her gauze robes, dancing, and the Greek who had accosted her. He had received a knife in his side for attempting to protect his wife.

He seemed to remember, vaguely, that she had called his name and that he had felt her kisses on his hand. Or was that a dream?

He turned his head weakly. He called: 'Sandra! Sandra!'

Then through the dimly lighted room came a tall girl with golden hair and a white, smiling face. His pulses jerked unpleasantly. Dorothy Mitchell! What was she doing here?

Dorothy came and knelt beside the bed.

'Oh, thank heaven, you are better,' she whispered.

'What are you doing here?' he asked sharply. 'Where is — my wife?'

'She was here a little while ago,' said Dorothy Mitchell. 'She sent for me. As soon as I came she left.'

'Why? Why did she send for you?' Michael asked feverishly.

'She said you would want me,' said Dorothy in a demure voice ... 'And also said she had no wish to stay and be sick-nurse. It was a job I could do, and I was to tell you she was going on with the divorce as quickly as possible and she hoped this business would teach you not to go round to these cafés after her.'

Michael lay rigid, breathing quickly.

It was a crushing disappointment to him. Somehow he had expected to find Sandra here . . . he had thought she was changed ... tender ... weeping over him. But he was a fool. He had been delirious, dreaming.

Dorothy shot her final bolt.

'And her last words before she went out were that I was to tell you she was leaving Cairo almost at once and you won't see her again.'

Michael like one mad with pain, mental pain, turned to Dorothy Mitchell, eyes gleaming.

'Get out — get out of my flat!'

'But Michael —' She shrank back.

'Get out, I say. If my wife has gone, you can go too. What you tell me may be true, but I don't trust you an inch and I don't believe a word you say. You've lied enough — done enough harm. Get out, I tell you, or I'll call my servants and have you thrown out!'

205

'But Michael — you need nursing —'

'Selim will nurse me.'

'Michael, I'm up against things — penniless —' She began to cry.

'It's your fault. You separated me from Sandra — you lied — you plotted. You can't do things like that without the price. Get out, I say!'

Dorothy Mitchell rose from her knees. She looked at Michael's livid face and glaring eyes, and shivered. This was no man to trifle with, no easy prey to trap. She had come up against the wrong person. She knew she was defeated — finally.

She left that flat in the early hours of the morning — a desperate woman. No money, no job, no hope of anything.

She returned to the small, cheap and rather dirty hotel where she had been living for the last week or two. She was sobbing, hysterical, when she entered her room. She knew she need never make another attempt to win Michael. It was over and done with. True, she had sent Sandra away tonight, and widened the breach between husband and wife. But it hadn't done her, Dorothy Mitchell, much good.

A wave of awful depression and despair came over her. Remorse for what she had done; horror at the prospect of being stranded ... an English girl in Cairo ... open to insults from natives ... to end, finally, in some charitable institution.

She saw a small blue bottle on her washstand; a strong disinfectant marked 'poison'.

A fit of frenzy possessed her, drove reason from her brain. She uncorked the bottle and poured the contents down her throat. The next instant she was writhing and shrieking, clutching at her throat.

The whole hotel wakened ... a crowd rushed up to the room whence came those terrible piercing screams.

Half an hour later the body of Nurse Dorothy Mitchell was conveyed to the mortuary. The unfortunate girl was dead. She had killed herself, died in torment. Yet not before she had made what reparation she could for her sins. For she sent a signed letter to Michael, admitting that she had planned to separate him from his wife and acknowledging the fact that he was absolutely innocent of any intrigue with her.

That letter was opened and read by Michael two days later. He was still in bed, stiff, sore and bandaged. When Nurse Mitchell's letter reached him, he wanted desperately to show Sandra. And the question was how to find Sandra. He had sent Selim, his boy, to the Café of a Thousand Stars and the boy returned to say that Sandra the Dancer had vanished. Hassan Bayout knew nothing but that she had packed up, taken her baby and left her rooms. Madame had some idea that Sandra meant to go home.

'Home' meant England.

Michael was distraught. If Sandra and the child went to England, how on earth would he ever trace them? He wanted to tell her that the poor, wretched nurse, Dorothy Mitchell, had died and exonerated him. It was only fair to himself that she should know.

Dr. Paige told him it would be madness for him to move for at least ten days. His wound was healing, but it must be given a chance.

So Michael stayed in bed, nursed by the devoted Selim, and fretted and fumed and wondered what had happened to his wife and child.

It was not that he had any particular hope of becoming reconciled to Sandra. So much had happened to antagonise her; to drive her away from him. But he wanted her to know, at least, that he had not been so dishonourable a cad as she had been made to believe. For their baby's sake he wanted her to know that.

It was ten full days before Paige allowed him to get up. Then he found himself so weak that it meant another two or three days before he could go out.

His first action was to hire a car and drive to Sandra's old lodgings. There, Madame could tell him little more than she had told Selim, days ago.

'The lady made up her mind to go away — to leave Cairo,' she said. 'She packed up and got the dear baby ready and off she went. All white she was, and her eyes full of tears.'

Michael winced.

'Did she say anything to you, Madame?'

'No Monsieur, beyoud that she could bear Egypt no more and must get back to England.'

Michael could get nothing out of Madame. So, disconsolately he retraced his footsteps to his waiting car. A thin figure followed him; tugged at his arm.

'Excellency —'

Michael turned and saw a miserable, half-starved looking lad of about twelve. He was Madame's servant. He was neglected and under-fed.

'What do you want?' asked Michael.

'You want to know where the lady is who lived here?' said the boy, eyeing him slyly.

Michael flushed.

'Do you know?'

'Yes. Give some piastres and I'll tell you,' said the boy.

Michael pulled out a handful of silver. 'Tell me then — quickly — for heaven's sake,' he said.

Sandra had left the French woman's house in Heliopolis two days after Michael was injured in the café. She had been so shocked, so disappointed in her discovery of Dorothy Mitchell in Michael's flat that night when she had given him all her care, her love, she had decided that she must leave Cairo — break away from this life, finally and absolutely.

She had not nearly enough money for her fare. But she had made up her mind to sink pride in this case and take it out of the bank. She knew, for a fact, money had been placed to her credit by Michael. She would draw on that account this time, and never again. Once she was home — amongst old friends who would give her and her baby a helping hand — she would get a job and return the money.

She went, therefore, to the bank and

drew out her money; sufficient for the fare, for clothes for a flight home, and a little margin for their keep when she first got home.

But fate stepped in and prevented her from taking the first available plane for home. She awoke on the very morning when she should have left Cairo, to find baby feverish and fretful. A doctor hastily called into the hotel where Sandra was staying, strongly advised Mrs. Hunt not to travel until the baby's temperature was down.

And so it was that Michael was in time. The native boy had been able to tell him that Mrs. Hunt drove from his employer's house to the bank. There he found out Sandra's hotel. Frantic with worry, Michael supposed he was much too late. But at the Station Hotel, to his surprise and delight, he found Sandra.

They faced each other again, these two, in her room at the hotel. And Michael, suddenly feeling very weak, sank into a chair. Whereupon Sandra, instead of being bitter and frozen, ran to him, looked anxiously at his pale, sharpened face and said :

'Oh — you're ill — your wound — is it well — ought you to be up?'

'I'm all right — only an attack of faintness,' he assured her. 'The wound is healed. Paige gave me leave to come out. Sandra, I've had a terrible time trying to trace you, and it was only by a lucky chance that boy heard you tell the driver to go to my bank.'

She looked down at him, her face flushing, her slim form trembling with sudden nervous excitement.

'Why did you trouble? What did you want with me? Isn't Dorothy Mitchell—'

'Dorothy Mitchell is dead, Sandra.'

'Dead!' she echoed, startled.

'Yes, and before she died, the unfortunate girl signed this confession and they sent it to me from the hospital. Will you read it?'

Sandra read what Dorothy Mitchell had dictated in her dying agony. And when she realised that Michael was absolutely innocent, that it was Dorothy who had plotted the whole thing and lied from start to finish, a great load was taken from her. She handed the paper back to her husband, her dark eyes full of tears.

'Oh, Michael ... what can I say? And I believed the worst of you!' she said brokenly.

Suddenly, he held out his arms, saying huskily: 'Oh, my dear, but I've believed the worst of you so many times. We can't go on like this, Sandra, we can't. I love you still. I've got to tell you so. I love you more than I ever did in London or Paris! My dear, my dearest, if you must leave Egypt and go home — then let me come, too.'

Reconciliations are happy things ... but perhaps the happiest moment of Sandra's whole life was some weeks later when she and her husband and baby reached England.

A letter came to Michael from his sister Elsie. A letter enclosing another, faded, crumpled-looking one with the words 'To my wife' written upon it in Hugh Lancaster's handwriting.

Elsie Lancaster told her brother that a very curious thing had happened. Apparently, Hugh had written this letter the night before he shot himself. He had put it in the drawer of a writing desk in his studio. The letter had slipped between the top and bottom drawer and never been discovered until long after his tragic death — quite recently in fact, when the desk went to be repaired, and the envelope was found.

In the letter to his wife, Hugh Lancaster told her that he was heavily in debt, and that it was financial trouble which had depressed him to such an extent that he could no longer bear life.

I've been in love with a Chelsea girl named Sandra, and she would not look at me. She was a decent little soul and I don't blame her. As a matter of fact I think Sandra one of the best. But I can't stand all these bills. They're driving me

215

insane. Forgive me, Elsie, if I do something desperate ...

That was only part of the long, tragic letter from the unhappy man. When Michael read it, he was too ashamed to look at his wife; too deeply moved to speak. He sat with his head between his arms. It was she who put an arm about him and whispered:

'Dearest — what does it matter? We're happy now.'

'But I misjudged you — I was brutal to you — I denied our love — almost wrecked it by my cruelty,' he said. 'Sandra, nothing I can do will ever make up for it.'

But she, with her lovely eyes shining, slipped her arms about his neck and said:

'Hush darling. Nothing matters now. I'm glad you know the truth about Hugh. But let's forget it. Let's only remember how happy we are now — you and I and Mary.'

In sudden passion of remorse, Michael crushed her to his heart.

'My love, my devotion are yours for ever, Sandra darling' he said.

And woman-like, she smiled through her tears and whispered:

'I love you, Michael! Kiss me!'